Peace, It's Wonderful

By William Saroyan

THE DARING YOUNG MAN ON THE FLYING TRAPEZE

INHALE AND EXHALE

THREE TIMES THREE

LITTLE CHILDREN

LOVE, HERE IS MY HAT

THE TROUBLE WITH TIGERS

A NATIVE AMERICAN

PEACE, IT'S WONDERFUL

P E A C E
It's Wonderful

William Saroyan

THE STARLING PRESS
432 FOURTH AVENUE, NEW YORK

Scarbrough
9.
12-5-55 rc
4-26-56 ccm

60

Printed in the United States of America

This book is for and against:

It is for the unnamed man in the multitude, whether he is scared to death, cowed, gathered into a mob, humiliated, fighting mad, unaware or indifferent.

It is against all men who, deliberately or unconsciously, with guilt or in innocence, out of nobility or stupidity, with regret or not with regret, are imposing death on the present world of helpless human beings.

Some of the stories in this collection have appeared in *Hairenik*, *The New Republic*, *The New Statesman & Nation*, *Story*, *Hinterland*, *The London Mercury*, *The Coast*, *The London Evening Standard*, *New Directions 1938*, *Inland Topics*, *College Humor*, and *Aperitif*.

CONTENTS

CONTENTS—*Continued*

Peace, It's Wonderful

The Greatest Country in the World

THE FATHER STARED at the fourteen-year-old boy with confusion and love, and tried his best to understand.

Joe, he said.

The boy was standing in front of the small mirror on the dining room wall, looking at the bad eye. He had just gotten up from the table without eating any of his supper. The boy's mother had put down her soup spoon and was leaning forward, eager and delighted about both of them.

The boy looked into the small mirror and back to the eyes of his father and mother.

What? he said. I just don't want any supper, that's all.

The father put his hand over his mouth and mustache thinking what he might say. He was fifty-five and this was his last son. This was the last of the five. The others had all gone away. Each had been a stranger to him, but from birth he had thought of this one as truly the son of himself. He remembered the baby smiling up at him from the crib, laughing silently, and year after year growing more and more like himself, as he had been as a boy in the old country. Now the boy was exactly his height, big like himself, with the same head and face, and the same thick blond hair.

The mother was an American, a girl Nick Frantisek had met in Pennsylvania thirty years ago when he had been working in the mines there and could barely speak two dozen words of English. She was still the girl he loved. He had never become unimpressed about her being an American, a very pretty American girl. The other sons had been either like her, or like the two of them, half and half. They had all been good boys, but this one had started out completely like himself. The boy's mother had been as pleased about that as the father. From the beginning she had learned enough Czech to please her husband and laugh with him intimately, as a foreigner in America, a Czech, a hunky workman, a simple man in a complex and crazy and magnificent new world. The others, the strangers, had pleased the foreigner; they had delighted him with the strangeness in them, even though they were his own; he had loved the Americantzi of their spirits; their amiability, their frankness, their innocence, and the spirit of their mother's tribe in each of them. He had tried to get each of them to learn a little Czech and each of them had done so, but it had always been a farcical thing to them, and to him, too. All they had done was roar with laughter when he had asked them in his deep voice what their names were, who their father was, and had expected them to answer with the foreign inflection and intonation. This they had done too, and added a few words of their own, and he and their mother and the kids had roared with delight. Joe, though, had really learned the language; he spoke it well, and seemed to *enjoy* speaking it, especially when only he and the old man were together.

The father had called out the boy's name as a Czech speaking to another, and at the mirror the boy had answered in English.

What? he had said. I just don't want any supper, that's all.

The father put his hand over his mouth and mustache and tried to think if he should speak in English or in Czech.

Joe, he said in English as if it were Czech, you eat it your sopper.

I'm not hungry, the boy argued.

Joe, the boy's mother said.

She wanted to say many things but couldn't say anything more than the boy's name. She wanted to say, Joe, you straighten out now, you crazy Joe, you.

Nick, the father, looked at the boy's mother and with a glance asked her not to speak. She answered the glance with a smile and began drinking her soup again. From his glance she could hear him saying, All right, Bess, *I* talk it to Joe.

The boy turned away from the mirror and looked at his father a moment, began to say something, changed his mind, and went over to the couch at the window and sat down, looking at the floor. Suddenly he said in Czech:

I'll kill them.

Joe, the father shouted at the boy.

The woman got up from the table and went upstairs.

She knew that this was a time Nick would want her to be out of the way.

Well, the boy said in English, they're not going to get by with anything like that with *me*.

Is that what you're still thinking about? the father said in Czech. I thought it was something else.

That's just part of it, the boy answered in Czech.

This pleased the father. He remembered his crazy fights with his own father in the old country, and the way they would turn out, the father right, the boy right, and a good free-for-all fight, with the rest of the men around, old and young, jumping in and shouting at them and holding them apart.

What's the rest of it? Nick said to the boy.

Well, Joe said, I guess I don't like—

He stopped talking and grew tense with a fury of hatred he had been trying all evening to control. As he sat in silence his father tried to understand what had happened, as Joe had told him. The department store clerks were on strike and were picketing the department stores. Joe didn't know anything about it. They were marching up and down in front of The Emporium, talking against the store and asking people not to go in. Joe came from the office where he was office boy and went past the strikers into the store. He bought the stuff he had been sent to get by the boss and left the store. All of a sudden four of them ran after him, knocked the package out of his hands, and began to beat him up. Joe had been so surprised he hadn't had a chance to do anything and by the time the men had been stopped by two cops, Joe had been pushed around and hit and hadn't done anything about it.

Ever since he had wanted to go back and fight the whole gang of them. His left eye was swollen and dark.

That's nothing, Nick said. They're workers fighting for rights. They made a mistake. You forget that, Joe.

The boy came out of his trance of anger and looked at his father.

I'll get those guys, he said.

I tell you no, Nick said.

The boy was silent a moment. He was thinking of the Germans, and the four men who had beaten him up.

Well, look at Germany he said. Who the hell do they think they are, trying to move in on our little country?

The father was delighted, but just as angry about Germany as the boy.

They'll go right in and take the whole country, the boy said.

They've got lots of trouble coming, Nick said to the boy in Czech. They can't beat the Czechs when the Czechs haven't got guns, let alone when they have got them.

They won't *use* guns, the boy said. They'll just bluff and take the whole country.

The old man got up from his chair and filled his chest with the blood of his youth, hating the small world and its wretched way of behaving.

Joe, he said. The Czechs will fight it the whole world. Them England. Them France.

What can a small country do? the boy said.

Small country? the father roared, and upstairs the mother heard him. Czecho-Slovakia is the biggest country in the world, she heard him shout.

You're crazy, Pa, the boy said.

Crazy? the old man shouted. You listen it to me, Joe.

He went over to the boy and towered over him with the crazy Slavic strength of his youth. The strength that had sent him from the village of Pribor to New York thirty-three years ago.

I tell you, he said, *my* country is the greatest country in the world.

The boy got to his feet, knowing there was going to be trouble, not so much between Germany and his father's country, but between his father and himself; knowing his father would be disgusted with him if he did not accept the trouble, and that he himself would be disgusted.

Czecho-Slovakia is a little tiny country, the boy said. Pretty soon it won't be a country at all.

He hated to know this, but he believed it was true because of the way of the world. The greatest country in the world was not the country whose men were great, it was the country with the *most* men. One man at a time maybe Czecho-Slovakia was the greatest country in the world, or at least one of the greatest, but that didn't go when it came to war or politics because when it was war or politics they didn't bother about the greatness of the men of the country, the greatness in each man; they just counted them and acted accordingly—the country with the most men fighting and winning a war or making demands and having them satisfied. That was all. It was too bad, but it was the truth and there was nothing his father could do about it.

The father was terribly angry about what the boy had said. He knew it was closer to the truth than what he was saying, but he didn't like it.

He began to roll up his shirt sleeve, the same as he'd done thirty years ago when there was an argument between himself and some other hunky, or anybody else.

Joe knew what this meant and got ready.

You say that? the father said.

Yes, the boy said.

Joe, the father said, I gonna fight it you.

Upstairs the American girl, the mother, listened to the crazy, absurd, magnificent argument, and a moment later she listened to the ridiculous and beautiful fight. At first she wanted to hurry downstairs and stop the fight, but after a moment she decided it would be better to wait a while. The fight started slowly, but after less than a minute it was a real fight, and she could hear the furniture getting pushed out of the way. She waited until she believed most of the furniture in the dining room had been ruined, and then went downstairs and stood in the doorway, watching them.

The father had a headlock on the boy, and the boy had some sort of a toe-hold on the father, and the two of them were turning about on the floor. The chairs were all knocked down, and everything that had been on the table was on the floor, the dishes broken and soup all over the rug. It was the loveliest-looking mess the girl had seen in over eight years, when the next to the youngest boy, Tom, had had a fight with Nick.

The girl was not at all displeased that Nick, her lover, was hardly getting the worst of it. In fact, she was flattered. As for her boy Joe, he was all right. He was fine. She remembered her visits to the Zoo and how the lions quarreling had always made her laugh and feel delighted. This was no different from the beautiful lions quarreling, and suddenly stopping and going right on living together in the cage. It was the same thing.

First the father and then the son forced his way to the top, and then the other became angry, just like the lions, and took command. Joe got his head free, but just as he did so Nick got his leg free and suddenly they were both on their feet, breathing freely and eager to start again. The father took the son around the waist and lifted him off the floor, but the son forced the father backward and down. On the floor Nick swiftly wrapped his arm around the boy's head again, and this time kept his legs down and out of reach. Joe was almost, but not quite, helpless.

Now, the father said, What you say, Joe?

The boy busted out laughing.

You're crazy, Pa, he shouted.

The old man lifted the boy and in a fury pushed him backward and against the wall. The noise was beautiful to the girl, and she loved the splendid way the whole house shook. The boy bumped his head, worked his neck, and was again free.

But this time the fight was over. The boy simply didn't go on fighting, and with no doubt at all about anything, at home, or in Europe, the old man turned, saw the girl smiling, and began to pick up the broken dishes.

Everything was all right. The Germans had a lot of trouble coming.

The boy picked up the chairs and put them in their places.

You remember that, Joe, the father said.

You're crazy, Pa, the boy said.

That's all right, Nick said. You know what I said.

The girl joined the two, mopping up the spilled soup with a dish cloth.

Thirty years ago they'd all said she was crazy to fall in love with a big bohunk, but now more than ever she knew how wrong they had been, and how right everything in the world had been when she had first kissed him.

The hunky turned to his girl and said, Fix the table again, Bess. Now we all gonna sit it down and eat it our sopper, and Joe and the girl busted out laughing at the crazy beautiful way he spoke, and was.

After supper the boy said quietly, *This* is the greatest country in the world, Pa, and the old man didn't bother to deny it.

The Insurance Salesman, the Peasant, the Rug Merchant, and the Potted Plant

ARSHAG GOROBAKIAN was a small man who earned his living as a salesman for the New York Life Insurance Company. He worked exclusively among his own people, the Armenians. In twenty years, he often told a new client, I have sold three hundred policies, and so far two hundred of my clients have died. He did not utter this remark with sorrow and it was not intended to be a commentary on the sadness of life. On the contrary, Gorobakian's smile indicated that what he meant by two hundred of them dying was simply that these were men who had cheated death of its awful victory, and at the same time made a monkey out of the New York Life Insurance Company. All shrewd men, he often told a new client. Men like yourself, in all things practical and brilliant. They said to themselves, Yes, we shall die, there is no way out of that, let us face the facts.

Here the insurance salesman would bring the printed charts and statistics out of his inside coat pocket and say, Here are the facts. You are forty-seven years of age, and by the grace of God in good health. According to the facts you will be dead in five years.

He would smile gently, sharing with the new client the thrill of dying in five years and earning thereby an enormous sum of money. In five years, he would say, you will have paid my company three hundred and eighty-seven dollars, and on dying you will have earned twenty thousand dollars, or a net profit of nineteen thousand six hundred and thirteen dollars.

That, he would say, is a fair profit on any investment.

Once, however, he talked to a peasant in Kingsburg who didn't believe he would be dead in five years.

Come back in seventeen or eighteen years, the peasant said.

But you are sixty-seven years old now, the insurance salesman said.

I know, the peasant said. But I shall not be swindled in an affair like this. I shall be alive twenty years from now. I have planted three hundred new olive trees and I know I shall not be dead until they are full grown. Not to mention the mulberry trees, and the pomegranate trees, and the walnut and almond trees.

No, the peasant said, the time is not ripe for a bargain of this sort. I know I shall be alive twenty years from now. I can feel it in my bones. Shall I say something?

Yes, the insurance salesman said.

I shall live *thirty* years longer, not twenty. You will admit I should be cheated in a deal of this sort.

The insurance salesman was small, courteous, quiet-spoken, and never aggressive.

I can see, he said, that you are a man of giant strength—

Giant strength? the peasant roared. Shall I say something?

The insurance salesman nodded.

What you say is the truth, he said. I am a man of giant strength. What death? Why should I die? For what reason, countryman? I am in no hurry. Money? Yes. It is good. But I am not going to die.

The insurance salesman smoked his cigar calmly, although inwardly he was in a state of great agitation, like a routed cavalry officer trying desperately to round up his men and organize another offensive.

Death to you? he said to the peasant. God forbid. In all my life I have never wished another man's death. Life is what we enjoy. The taste of the watermelon in the summer is the thing we cherish.

May I say something? the peasant interrupted.

Again the insurance salesman nodded.

What you say is true, he said. The thing we cherish is the taste of the watermelon in the summertime. And bread and cheese and grapes in the cool of evening, under the trees. Please go on.

I do not wish any man's departure from this warm scene of life, the insurance salesman said. We must face the facts, however.

He shook the documents in his hand.

Our world is a crazy world, he said. You are a strong man. You enjoy the taste of the watermelon. You are walking in the city. An automobile strikes you and where are you? You are dead.

The peasant frowned.

Ah, yes, he said. The automobile.

In the event that you are killed accidentally, which God forbid, the insurance salesman said, you will be rewarded doubly.

The confounded automobiles, the peasant said. I shall be very careful in the streets.

We are all careful, the insurance salesman said, but what good does it do us? More people are killed every year in automobile accidents than in one year of a great war.

May I say something? the peasant said.

Say it, the insurance salesman said.

I have half a mind to be protected, the peasant said. I have half a mind to take out an insurance policy.

That is a wise plan, the insurance salesman said.

The peasant purchased a policy and began making payments. Two years later he called the insurance salesman to his house and reprimanded him severely, although politely. He complained that although he had spent several hundred dollars, he had not so much as come anywhere near being killed, which he considered very odd.

I do not want the policy any longer, he said.

The insurance salesman told the ironic story of another man who gave up his policy after two years, and three weeks later was gored to death by an angry bull. But the peasant was not impressed with the story.

May I say something? he said. There is no bull in the world strong enough to gore me. I would break his neck. No thank you, I do not want to be insured. I have made up my mind not to die, even for a profit. I have had a hundred chances of walking in front of an automobile, but always I have stepped back cautiously and allowed it to go by.

That was fourteen years ago, and the peasant, a man named Hakimian, is still alive.

The insurance salesman, however, preferred people more enlightened than peasants. He himself was a graduate of college. His preference was for men with whom he could talk for hours about other things, and then little by little move in with the insurance speech. He would often drive two hundred miles to San Francisco to talk with a dentist who had graduated from college.

Once he decided to drive his Buick across the country to Boston. It was a journey of ten days. Along the way there would be much to see, and in Boston he would visit his sister and her husband and their eleven children. He drove to Boston, visited his sister and her family, and met a rug merchant who was a college graduate. Three times in ten days he called at this man's home and carried on pleasant conversations. The man's name was Haroutunian and he was extremely fond of conversation. The insurance salesman found him brilliant on all subjects. But when the subject of life insurance was introduced he discovered that his friend was, bluntly, in no mood for it. At least, not for the present.

The time came for the insurance salesman to return to California. Before departing he was paid a visit by the rug merchant, Haroutunian, who was carrying a small potted plant.

My friend, the rug merchant said, I have a brother in Bakersfield which is near where you live. I have not seen him in twenty years. Will you do me a favor?

Of course, the insurance salesman said.

Carry this plant to my brother with my greetings, the rug merchant said.

Gladly, the insurance salesman said. What plant is this?

I do not know, the rug merchant said, but the leaf has a wonderful odor. Smell it.

The insurance salesman smelled the plant and was disappointed in the smell of the leaf.

It is truly a heavenly smell, he said.

The rug merchant gave the insurance salesman the name and address of his brother, and then said:

One more thing. The agricultural department in each state demands that a plant being transported be examined for plant insects. There are none on this plant, but the law is the law. You will have to stop a minute at the agricultural department of each state. A formality.

Oh, the insurance salesman said.

His word had been given, however, so he put the plant into his car and made his departure from Boston.

He was a very law-abiding man and the plant caused

him quite a little trouble. Very often even after he had found the agricultural department of each state, the inspector was out of town and wouldn't be back for several days.

The result of the whole thing was that the insurance salesman got home in twenty-one days instead of ten. He drove a hundred miles to Bakersfield and found the rug merchant's brother.

The plant was safe and was now growing small red blossoms that gave off an odor which to the insurance salesman was extremely unpleasant.

Three thousand six hundred and seventy-eight miles I have carried this wonderful plant, the insurance salesman said, from the home of your brother in Boston to your home in Bakersfield. Your brother sends greetings.

The rug merchant's brother liked the plant even less than the insurance salesman did.

I do not want the plant, he said.

The insurance salesman was a man who was hardly ever amazed by anything. He accepted the brother's indifference and took the plant home with him.

He planted it in the finest soil in his back-yard, bought fertilizer for it, watered it, and took very good care of it.

It is not the plant, he told a neighbor. It nauseates me. But some day I shall perhaps be going back to Boston to visit my sister and when I see the rug merchant again I know he shall ask about the plant and I shall be pleased to tell him that it is flourishing. I feel that I have as good a chance as any man to sell him an insurance policy some day.

The Year of Heaven

THERE IS A whole year of my life that's not included in
the years I've been alive. It is a year that is back there in
the days of the streets, and while the *real* year that year
was like the one before, 1916, and the one after, 1918,
another year took place at the same time and was more or
less lost for ten or eleven years. Then I dreamed the movie
and got it back.

It was a wonderful year, that separate year of 1917.
It was the year of the movies. It was the year in which
I left the world and went to heaven in the picture theaters.
That was the only time I ever went to heaven and I went
in rags, as it were, and by foot. I went with a dirty face,
not a face glowing with holy light; and sometimes I went
with a face wet with the rain of winter; with hands cold
and dirty; sometimes even my shoes would be wet, all soft,
and my coat too.

The movie was the one of the world, the one that never
ended. It was the dream being dreamed, outside in the
city, in the dirt and rain, and inside in the picture theater,
in the darkness, with the pictures moving in front of you,

the pipe organ saying how it was, and the dream unfolding in front of you until you got up and walked right into it and on into heaven, with Theda Bara and Mary Pickford, William Farnum and Two-Gun Hart, Fatty Arbuckle and Charlie Chaplin, and all the others who were in heaven in those days.

That year in heaven I forgot after the Armistice, and then one night while I was dreaming I dreamed the movie again and the whole year came back to me. It was a bright day in the dream and I was back in the streets selling papers and everybody was buying them, instead of not buying them, the way it had been in 1917. Everybody was buying them and I think I made a dollar and forty cents in no time.

I'm dreaming, I said in the dream. It wasn't a bright day: it was raining. They didn't buy any papers either. All it did was rain and the people hurried home. I went to George Koriakle's on Eye Street and traded a paper for four chunks of fudge. I ate the fudge and then went over to the Liberty Theater and gave Joe a paper and he let me in free. I went in just as Jimmy Valentine jumped up onto the chandelier. I'd seen the picture four times in the last four days and knew the story by heart. It didn't stop being heaven, though, because Jimmy Valentine, although once a safe-cracker, was at heart a man of great nobility, and when the girl got locked in the safe accidentally, Jimmy rubbed his fingers on stone until they bled and then when his fingers were sensitive that way he went to work and cracked that safe and saved the girl.

That year is the year I began to get over cowboy

pictures. If they were being shown I'd see them through, of course, but I didn't like them. I liked comedies, but especially the ones with Snub Pollard in them, and a young zany named Al St. Joy. I liked love stories too. I liked the outdoor ones where the girl would be somebody wonderful and good like Mary Pickford and it seemed like the whole world was against a little kid like that with nothing but goodness in her heart, and then it would happen, the little girl's goodness would knock hell out of all the viciousness and she'd get the bad ones put in jail where they belonged. And all like that.

Before I got over cowboy stories, they were the best. The way to do it was with a gun. Draw quickly, fire accurately, duck and, if hurt, fall slowly, and go on firing. The worst it would ever be would be a flesh wound that would never keep you from getting on the horse and riding across the plains to the small house, leaping off the horse, stamping across the porch just in time for her to run out of the house into your arms, crying, O Danny, Danny. I didn't exactly see through that stuff. It was simply that I couldn't get a horse and even if I could buy a gun, I wouldn't know who to use it on, might not be able to shoot accurately, might be slow on the draw, might get shot through the head instead of through the flesh of my left leg, above the knee, and might accidentally shoot somebody who wasn't guilty.

The streets in our city were pretty much paved and nobody seemed to be arriving on horseback anyway, and I never saw anybody carrying a gun, except the cops, who were being paid to do it. And I never saw a cop draw a gun and do anything about anything. I saw a guitar-player of a marimba band draw a pistol in front of the Sequoia Hotel and wave it at the five other members of the band and a white woman, but he didn't fire, and I didn't know what it was all about. One of the other boys coaxed him into putting the gun back into his pocket and they all went into the lobby of the hotel as if nothing had happened.

So it didn't seem as if a gun would be any good. The only thing that seemed to be any good at all was wit, daring and forthrightness. But most important of all was virtue. If you had all the wit in the world, and a lot of daring and plenty of forthrightness, but no virtue, you were still on the wrong side and no good.

All I did that year was turn away from the city and walk into the theater and on into heaven. There was nowhere else to go. It was a year of London, New York, War, Love, Comedy, Newsreels and Heaven. It got so I didn't even think the newsreels were real. It got so I thought they were part of the movie too, the pictures of soldiers marching, and Generals striding about mechanically, turning feverishly, their lips moving, their arms rising and falling like the arms of men made of machinery. It couldn't be anything more than a movie. It was all part of the dream. The people walking along country roads, carrying small bundles, leaving bombed villages. It was all part of the great endless moving picture. The wounded in hospitals, with Royalty and Actresses and Generals going around mechanically from one bed to another, nodding, bowing, shaking hands and all that stuff.

The trains going with all the faces looking out, and the others, not going, waving. If it wasn't a movie, I didn't know what it was.

It got so that even outside of the theater it was all a movie. Even *I* was one of the unnamed ones in the movie. One of the faces you saw for just a moment among a hundred faces.

I forgot about that strange year until I dreamed the movie and it had stopped raining and there seemed to be a sudden absence of miserliness and error in the world.

I guess the people will always be leaving the world and going to heaven. There's really nowhere else to go.

The Europa Club

In 1918 one of the gambling joints I used to loaf around in, pretending to be selling papers, was The Europa Club on Tulare Street, across the Southern Pacific tracks, near China Alley, in Chinatown.

The Europa Club was supposed to be a gambling joint, but actually it was nothing more than a place where men with no money sat around and talked, and during the War I used to walk over to Chinatown and visit this place. The ugliest men in the world were loafing in The Europa Club in 1918. Italians, Greeks, Negroes, Chinese, Japs, Hindus, Russians, and Americans. Every kind of American, from big dumb Indians and sad-eyed Mexicans to old white-trash gamblers from Texas.

The place was full of tables and chairs and spittoons. There was a player-piano in a corner, a bar along the back wall, and over the mirror was an oil painting of a man who looked a little like Woodrow Wilson. It was a great big painting, the work, no doubt, of a loafer who had painted it for drinks.

The place stank. The air was polluted with the wasted

hours of many men, and every time I went into the place
with a dozen papers under my arm I used to try to figure
out what kept them going. I used to figure maybe it was
the silent player-piano in the corner. Maybe they were
waiting for some spendthrift to show up and drop a nickel
in the slot. Maybe the men were waiting for music. Or
maybe it was the big painting of Woodrow Wilson, the
great man of the bad years. Maybe it was the dumb force
within themselves, centuries old, demanding to grow centuries older. Maybe it was nothing.

One day the little Jap called Suki swallowed a big fly.

He was a very melancholy-looking man. Any Jap
who is loafing is a melancholy-looking man because it's not
in that race to loaf. He was disgusted with everything,
and nobody would be his friend. He tried to get along
with his countrymen who were loafing in the dump, but
they wouldn't have anything to do with him. He tried to
laugh with the Negroes, but he couldn't laugh that way,
and they didn't like the disharmony of his giggle mingling
with their guffaws. They bawled him out every time he
tried to laugh with them. He tried to be friendly with the
Indians and the Mexicans. But *nobody* wanted to be
friendly with him, so he gave it up and just sat in a corner.

One day in August Suki noticed that everybody in the
room was aware of the flies. Not bothered; just aware. It
was very hot and very still in the room and the big flies
were flying around and lighting on noses and making the
noise flies make. Suki got up from his chair and waved at
a couple of them and didn't catch one. Everybody noticed
him. He waved at another group of flies and this time

caught one. The fly was furious and tried to get away, buzzing loudly, but Suki held it by its wings.

Then he swallowed it.

His countrymen went over to him and spoke in Japanese with great dignity and great seriousness. It seemed they wished to know why he had swallowed the fly. He told them he had swallowed the fly because he was going crazy, from loafing. His countrymen were very upset and at the same time very proud. They thought at first that he was showing off. He had no labor to perform in the world, he said sadly. They asked what labor he wished to perform, and he said he wished to plant and care for strawberries. They told him the season for the growing of strawberries was ended long ago. He said he knew that.

His countrymen told the other loafers why Suki had swallowed the fly.

For weeks during the last days of the War the loafers at The Europa Club talked about Suki and the fly he swallowed. Part of the time they looked upon him as a fool and part of the time as a hero.

Before the War ended, Suki swallowed four flies. I saw him swallow the first one and the last one. The Negroes told me about the others. They said he liked flies. They roared with laughter about Suki and the flies.

He was a very melancholy-looking man.

The loafers waited patiently, and at last the War ended.

When the soldiers of our town came back from the War, The Europa Club was sold to a soldier who kicked out the loafers and put the place in order. The soldier himself dropped nickels into the slot of the pianola and every time I walked into the place I heard music. Men were at the tables, really gambling, for money. At the bar were men who were drinking. It was all illegal and all that, but the soldier was a hard guy and he knew all the ropes. His best friends were cops.

One afternoon in February while I was in The Europa Club I saw Suki come in and buy a drink. He was disgusted, and after he swallowed the drink, he caught a fly and swallowed it. The soldier almost went out of his head when he saw Suki swallow the fly. He took Suki by the neck with his left hand and by the seat of the pants with his right hand and lifted him out into the street.

The little Jap walked away without turning around.

The soldier came back in and dropped another nickel into the slot.

Then he turned around and saw me.

I want you to get the hell out of this place, and stay out, he said.

1924 Cadillac For Sale

ANY TIME YOU think you can go out and pull something over on somebody, like selling them a bad used car, you're kidding yourself because people don't believe lies any more unless they've got their heart set on having the used car anyway. I used to sell an average of two used cars a week five years ago, but nowadays I'm lucky if I don't sell two a day. People who buy used cars these days would kill anybody who tried to stop them from buying. They just naturally want a used car. I used to try to argue them into believing they *ought* to have a used car, but that was before I found out I was wasting my time. That was before I found out people don't like to be fooled any more.

All I do now is hang around this used car lot and wait for people to come around and start asking questions about the jalopies we're showing.

I tell them the truth.

I let them know exactly what they're getting, but it don't seem to stop them any when they've got their hearts set on going for a ride in an automobile. They just naturally insist on making a down payment and driving away. It used to make me feel real proud and smart to sell a used car in the old days, but nowadays I feel a little hurt every time somebody comes up and forces me to sell him one of these out-of-date broken-down heaps. I feel kind of useless and unnecessary, because I know I ain't selling anybody *anything*. I'm just letting the tide of humanity rush where it pleases or must.

They come here by the hundreds every day, men, women, and children, wanting a used car, and all I do is let them have their way. I don't put up any kind of an argument, because it's no use. An old lady who doesn't know how to drive a car wants to buy an old Hupmobile because it's green, so why should I interfere with her wishes? I let her know the truth about the old heap, but she buys it anyway, and the next day I see her going down the street forty-three miles an hour. She's in sports clothes, and the radio's going full blast, with a crooner hollering: *Deep in the heart of me.*

My God, it's beautiful and awful.

And then again a small boy, no more than twelve, comes in here with eleven dollars he's saved up, and he wants to know how much is the cheapest car on the lot; and I show him that 1922 Chevrolet we've been offering for fifteen dollars for seven years now, and he hops in, holds the wheel and says he'll go home and get the other four dollars. He comes back with his big brother, who signs the papers for him, and the next thing I know they've got the hood lifted and they're repairing the motor. In my opinion the old heap's got no more chance of moving than a bronze horse in a park; but three hours later something happens, and the whole lot is full of smoke and noise.

It's the old Chevrolet.

By the time the smoke clears I can see them walloping down the street, and I know deep in the heart of me, as the song goes, that either the people of this country are natural-born heroes or that the average used car, for all any of us knows, is part human and will respond to tender and loving care, just as anything else will.

There was a young Filipino came in here last April who'd been doing farm work down around Bakersfield, and he'd saved up a small amount of money which, he said, I wish to purchase a sports model Packard touring car with. Well, I had that great big battleship of a Packard that had been abandoned in the middle of the desert just south of Pixley about seven years ago, and I didn't want to see the boy gypped, so I told him I didn't have a sports model Packard touring car except one old one that had something fundamentally wrong with the motor and wouldn't run.

You wouldn't be interested in that car, I said.

I would appreciate it very much if you would allow me to look at it, the Filipino said.

His name was Vernon. I'm telling you this because I remember how amazed I was when he signed the papers. Vernon Roxas. The other boys who sat in the car with him when he drove out of the lot had names that were

even worse.   One of the boys was called Thorpe; another
was named Scott, and another Avery.   My God, them
ain't names you ever see attached to people, native or
alien, and me hearing them little men calling each other
names like that made me stop in my tracks and wonder
what the world was coming to.   I mean I felt awful proud
of them young citizens.   I like people just so they're
sensible and honest and sincere, and I like Filipinos as much
as I like any other kind of people.   I was just profoundly
impressed by their superb adaptability.   Them boys had
not only adjusted themselves to our world: they'd fitted
themselves out in the best style of our clothes, and they'd
taken over our most impressive names.   I felt awful proud
of that condition in America among the boys from the
Island.

Of course I was a little worried about their wanting
that old Packard.

I showed the car to this boy Vernon Roxas, and he
began crawling all over the car, trying out everything but
the motor.

What is the price? he said.

Well, there was no price.   I'd never bothered to give it
a price because I was satisfied to have it in the lot as a sort
of decoy, just to take space.   I figured I'd do the boy a
favor and name a big price so he wouldn't buy it.

Well, I said, it's pretty expensive.   That'll run you
about $75.

You mean $75 dollars is the first payment? the boy
asked.

Well, right there I guess I could have swindled him, and for a moment I was tempted to do it; but I just couldn't go through with the idea.

No, I said; $75 is the total cost.

I'll take it, the boy said.

He brought all kinds of money from his pockets, and we counted. He had a little over $75. I drew up the papers, and he signed. He said he would come back later that afternoon with several of his friends. He'd take the car then.

He came back in two hours with eleven well-dressed Filipinos named Thorpe, Scott, Avery, and other names like that. Each of them was carrying a satchel containing tools and other stuff. Well, they took off their coats and rolled up their sleeves and went to work. One of them started working on the motor, and the others started working on other parts of the car. In less than two hours they had that old warship looking like the car the Governor rides around in when there's a parade. And they had smoke coming out of it too.

I mean they'd fought their battle and won.

I stood in the lot with my mouth open, because never before in my life had I seen such beautiful co-operation and strategy. They just naturally fell on that pile of junk and tightened and cleaned and greased and oiled until it looked like a five-thousand-dollar job. Then they all got into the car and slowly drove out of the lot with the motor barely making any sound at all, like the motor of a car just out of the factory.

I couldn't believe my eyes. Or my ears, either.

I walked beside the boy at the wheel, Vernon Roxas, while the car moved out of the lot.

Vernon, I said, you boys have just taught me the greatest lesson any man can learn.

It is our opinion, Vernon said, that this Packard will travel fifty thousand miles before its usefulness is exhausted.

Well, I said, I don't doubt it the least. I'm more or less convinced that it will keep moving as long as you boys want it to.

And don't ever think it's the car. Don't ever think its machinery. It's people. It's America, the awful energy of the people. It's not machinery, it's faith in yourself. Them boys from the Island went to work and changed that worthless heap of junk into a beautiful and powerful automobile with a motor that hummed.

When they drove out of this lot in that magnificent Packard my heart cheered this great country. People with no money having the polite impudence to want class and get it at no expense and to insist on getting it no matter how run-down and useless it might seem at first glance.

I don't *sell* used cars any more.

I just stand around in this lot and admire the will of the people, men, women, and children, as they take over a bankrupt and exhausted piece of machinery and breathe new and joyous life into it. I just stay here and admire this great and crazy race of adventure-loving people who can't be stopped by truth or expense. I just watch them throw themselves into a cause and come out with a roaring motor that five minutes ago was a piece of dead and rusted junk.

You're the first man who's come to this lot in six months and not *forced* me to sell him a car. I want to shake your hand. Like yourself I'm an honest man, and I believe as you do that every car in this lot is worthless, useless, and incapable of moving. I believe as you do that anybody who buys one of these cars is a fool and ought to have his head examined. It's my job to let the people have what they want, but I believe as you do that the most they can find here is junk, so naturally I admire somebody who agrees with me. This old 1924 Cadillac you've been looking at, in my opinion, isn't worth five cents, but we're asking sixty dollars for it. I don't think you're the type of man who could bring this car to life; and I wouldn't care to see you try, because if you failed I'd feel unhappy and maybe lose my faith in people.

But if you *want* to give it a try after all I've told you, well, that's your affair. I won't try to stop you. I'm telling you in all sincerity that this car is no good, but if you think you can fall on it like the others who buy cars here every day, and make it go, why go ahead. Nothing can amaze me any more, and if you've got your heart set on driving a Cadillac, well, here's a Cadillac, and good luck to you.

The Love Kick

LOTS OF PEOPLE in Coalinga don't like Clip Rye just because he kicked Miss Alice Pfister on Oilfield Street in
front of Joe Kolb's barber shop at high noon, but most of
them don't understand Clip. Any other place but a little
run-down town like this, Clip would be appreciated by
upper-class people, but what happens to him in this God-
forsaken neck of the woods? He's disgraced. He's in jail.
What the hell for? Because he done it. Because he busted
loose and let her have it. He kicked her. I ain't got nothing
against Miss Pfister or anybody like her, only I don't want
any truck with them kind of ladies, weekdays, Sundays,
or holidays. Clip busted loose and kicked her. Lots of
people don't like him.

The only trouble with Clip's kick was that it was a
love kick. A lady like Miss Pfister don't deserve a love
kick from a man like Clip, the most famous lover in
Tulare County. What I say is, he was too kind to her.

Let me tell you how it happened. Clip ain't no brother
of mine. He ain't no cousin of mine. We ain't even
close friends. I ain't prejudiced in Clip's favor and I ain't

one to say kicking a lady is exactly in keeping with the rules on how to behave in public. I kicked a lady once myself, and *nearly* kicked a dozen others. The lady I kicked claimed I was a loafer. She claimed I was lazy. My first wife. I didn't do it in public the way Clip did. You're the first man in the world knows I kicked a lady. I don't go around bragging about it because lots of people are sensitive on the subject and don't like to hear of a lady being kicked. Nine out of ten of them don't ever stop to think it over carefully. They just don't like the idea. I didn't want to kick my first wife. Not even after she almost drove me crazy nagging at me. She wanted me to take a correspondence course on how to increase the brain's capacity for thinking. My brain has a better than average capacity for thinking already, and I don't like it. I don't sleep good, on account of thinking. I keep thinking all the time. I think how different everything in the world would be if I had two or three hundred dollars. Then I start thinking along the political line, and I start thinking how wonderful it would be if I was a Senator or maybe Vice-President.

I'm thinking all the time, night and day, and my first wife had the impudence to ask me to take a correspondence course on how to increase the capacity of my overworked brain. Even then, though, I didn't *want* to kick her, my right leg just got out of control and the first thing I knew my first wife was sitting on the parlor floor calling me dirty names.

You may not believe me, but I'm still sorry about that. Ordinarily I'd only have clouted her, but my right leg got out of control. I apologized on the spot, but she wouldn't listen to me. She was mortified with shame. I told her I was sorry. I lifted my right leg to show her how out of control it was. She saw it trembling and aching to kick again, but she wouldn't understand. Honey, I said, it wasn't me, it was my leg. I didn't mean to do it.

She went right home to her mother and I never saw her again.

Clip Rye did it at high noon, though, and right in the street. A lot of people saw it happen. A lot of people were eye-witnesses. That's why they took Clip to jail. They claimed they not only saw it, they heard it. They claimed it made a lot of noise, especially when Miss Pfister sat down on the sidewalk.

Clip Rye is a natural-born lady-kicker. I reckon every man in the world is a natural-born lady-kicker if he'd be honest about it. I never yet knew a man who wasn't aching to kick some lady or other. I guess most men go through life keeping their right leg under powerful control. The average man wastes a Niagara of energy holding back his kicking leg.

What I say is, Kick a lady if it's the only thing to do. Let her have it.

For all we know, my friend, maybe the ladies themselves are asking for it. Maybe they want to be kicked. Maybe deep down inside they're just begging for a strong, healthy kick. I got a feeling Clip Rye's kick did Miss Pfister more good than harm. I just bet that kick was the starting point of a new era in Miss Pfister's love life.

Miss Pfister's love life is just about as interesting as the love life of the desert horned-toad. Miss Pfister ain't had a lover. She don't know what a man smells like. She ain't had a man's hands go over her the way a man's hands ought to go over a lady. Consequently, her love life has taken a half dozen special directions. First she was in the choir at the Presbyterian Church. Nothing happened. So she went over to the Baptist Church as a Sunday School teacher. Nothing happened. So she went in for astrology and studied the stars. Then she went in for professional gossiping. She spent all her time discussing the immorality of the people of Coalinga, especially Clip Rye, and the immorality of movie stars, and that's all she cared to do. She used up *most* of her energy talking about the immorality of Clip Rye, though. Every time she met Clip Rye in the street she lifted her nose at him.

She was flirting, of course. She was crazy about Clip Rye. Anybody but a fool could see how crazy Miss Pfister was about Clip Rye.

She acted as if she wouldn't look at Clip Rye if he was the last man in the world, but that was her way of flirting. Clip knew it, too. He knew what she wanted, even if she herself didn't, and Clip resented it. He didn't resent her gossiping about him, he resented her passion. It drove him crazy. That old hag's in love with me, he used to say.

Clip was sitting in Joe Kolb's barber shop getting a haircut. Last Saturday. He was minding his own business sitting there and staring out of the window at the people passing in the street. Then Miss Pfister went by in the street. Then she went by again, going up the street, and looking in at Clip and lifting her nose. I'm giving you the evidence. I'm trying to prove Clip don't deserve social ostracism. Then Miss Pfister went down the street, lifting her nose. Then up, then down, looking at Clip, adoring him, and lifting her nose, and then Clip's right leg got out of control and he jumped out of Joe Kolb's barber chair and ran out into the street and grabbed Miss Pfister by the arm. He was disgusted. Miss Pfister was so delighted she screamed. Clip bawled hell out of her. She bawled hell out of Clip. It sounded like a man and a woman who had been married sixteen years and knew all about one another, and Clip knew it and it burned him up. He was disgusted and sore and embarrassed. And then it was all over.

Miss Pfister was sitting in front of Joe Kolb's barber shop, on the sidewalk, at high noon, and everybody in town was running to the scene of the crime, and Miss Pfister didn't want to get up.

Clip was so sore he didn't know what to do. If Miss Pfister had gotten up he would have kicked her again, but she didn't get up. A couple of church-people started complicating Miss Pfister's love life, and the result of it was they had Clip Rye taken to jail and he's there yet and everybody in town is sore at him for kicking Miss Pfister.

Myself, I'd say Clip shouldn't have done it, if for no other reason than that it made Miss Pfister so happy. She didn't deserve such affection from a man like Clip Rye. I didn't see Clip kick her, but I showed up in time to hear Miss Pfister crying, and I know the kinds of crying there is, and Miss Pfister's kind was the joyous love variety.   She was just thrilled to tears.

So they took Clip Rye to jail.   They took him to jail for doing a noble kindness like that.

Joe Kolb never did get a chance to finish Clip's haircut.

Little Moral Tales From the Old Country

MY GRANDMOTHER LUCY, to illustrate the awful love
liness of faith in God and goodness, and the absurdity of
despair, tells the story of the carpenter of many hundreds
of years ago who, on his way home one evening, was
stopped by a friend who said, My brother, why are you
so down in face?

You too would feel as I do, the carpenter said, if you
were in my position.

What is it? his friend said.

By tomorrow morning, the carpenter said, I must have
eleven thousand eleven hundred and eleven pounds of fine
hardwood sawdust for the king or I will lose my head.

The carpenter's friend smiled and put his arm around
the carpenter's shoulders.

My friend, he said, be light of heart. Let us go eat and
drink and forget tomorrow. The great God shall remember for us while we worship.

So they went to the carpenter's home where they found
the carpenter's wife and children in tears. This was
stopped with eating, drinking, talking, singing, dancing,

and all manner of faith in God and goodness. In the midst of laughter, the carpenter's wife began to weep and said, So, my husband, in the morning you are to lose your head and we are all enjoying the goodness of life. So it's that way.

Remember God, the carpenter said, and the worship continued.

All night they celebrated and when light pierced darkness and it was day, everyone became silent and stricken with fear and grief. From the king came his men knocking softly at the door of the carpenter's house, and the carpenter said, Now I go to die, and opened the door.

Carpenter, they said, the king is dead. Build him a coffin.

II

My Uncle Aram, to illustrate any number of extraordinary things, tells the story of another king and another man. This king was given to ridiculous whims, and this man, one of his advisers, had more good sense, wit, and daring than the king and all his ancestors put together.

The king said one evening, By morning I want you to let me know how many blind there are in Constantinople.

Oh, the adviser said. Oh, I see.

He went away to think of a solution to this absurd assignment. He obtained the services of an expert bookkeeper, placed him on a fine horse, put a book and a pen in his hands, and told him to ride with him through the city and to put down the blind as they came to them.

With a strong rope, to the saddle of his horse, the adviser tied an enormous branch of a lilac tree, and dragging this behind him began to ride over the streets of the city.

After a moment a man in the street looked up and shouted, Mahmed, what are you doing?

The adviser turned to the bookkeeper and said, Bookkeeper, this man is blind. Begin your account.

On the next street a lady put her head out of a fine house and said, Young man, what are you doing? and the adviser told the bookkeeper to continue his account.

By morning the account of the blind included all the people of Constantinople and the adviser and the bookkeeper turned their horses into the gardens of the king's palace, still dragging the branch of the lilac tree.

The king himself came out onto a balcony and looked down at his adviser.

Hey, Mahmed, he shouted. What are you doing?

The adviser turned quickly to the bookkeeper and said, Bookkeeper, the account is now complete. This son of a bitch is blind too.

III

To ILLUSTRATE THE comic stupidity of people who get ahead of themselves in their ambitions and dreams, my uncle tells also the story of the two Arabs, one wise and one foolish, who went into the hills to shoot bears.

I have already sold the skin of my bear, the foolish one said. Have you sold yours?

No, the wise one said. I shall begin to think of that

after I have killed my bear. How is it that you are so confident?

Oh, the other said, it is simply that I am so expert at shooting, so wise in the ways of bears, and so shrewd in transactions.

They went far into the hills and broke away from one another. An enormous bear appeared from behind an enormous boulder in front of the foolish Arab who dropped his gun, fell to the ground, and pretended to be dead. The bear came up to him, smelled him all over, watered in his face, and then slowly walked away. When the bear was far away, the foolish Arab got up and dried his face. The other Arab came to him and said, What did the bear say to you?

The foolish one, who was now less foolish than he had been, said, The bear said, From now on don't sell my skin till you've got it off my body.

IV

BY WAY OF reprimanding two-faced people who speak well of a man to his face and libel him to others, he tells also the story of the bear and the man who were friends and went for a walk one day in the winter. The man stopped and blew on his hands and the bear said, My friend, why do you blow on your hands? To warm them, the man said. After their walk they went to the man's house for supper and when soup was served the man blew on it and the bear said, My friend, why do you blow on the soup? To cool it, the man said. The bear (in much the manner of an angry man, with the temperament of my uncle) roared, I revile that breath which blows both hot and cold.

V

To RETURN SMALL people with pretensions to greatness to their normal size, he tells also the story of the lion wounded by the bullet of a hunter, roaring with pain and on the verge of coming to death. Came the small slow-moving turtle to the lion and said, What is your pain? I have been shot by a hunter, the lion said. The turtle became angry and said, May the arms of such men be broken who come to injure magnificent creatures of the earth like us. Brother turtle, the lion said, let me tell you the injury of the hunter pains me less than what you have just said. And then the lion died.

On this same theme, he tells also the story of the flea in the elephant's ear as the elephant walked across a bridge. My friend, the flea said, when enormities like us cross a bridge it shakes with our mightiness.

VI

A HUSBAND AND WIFE were traveling by donkey over a mountain road to Bitlis when before them appeared a blind man groping for his way.

The husband said, God has given you two eyes; get down and walk and let the blind man ride.

The wife said, The blind take advantage; let us pass

by. But the husband had taken pity on the blind man
and wanted him to ride.

Look, he said. He is hurting his feet; get down and
let him ride.

So the wife got down and the blind man got up beside
the husband. The wife walked, the men rode and came at
last to the city.

The husband said, This is Bitlis; we will leave you here;
get down.

Get down? the blind man said. Just because you
guided my donkey for me through the hills, you want to
steal the animal?

The wife saw the trouble coming and groaned.

My foolish husband, she said.

Please get down, the husband said. I took pity on you
and carried you on my donkey to the city. Now go your
way.

The blind man began to shout. A crowd gathered.
The blind man spoke to the people. The husband saw
that the people were more in sympathy with the blind man
than with him, so he said to his wife, You were right; I
have made a mistake; let him have the donkey; let us go.

Yes, the wife said. Let us go.

The blind man called out, First you wanted to steal
my donkey; now you want to steal my wife; and my wife,
seeing a whole man, no longer wants a blind one.

The wife groaned with terror. The husband was
speechless.

The crowd believed the blind man. He was blind.
They pitied him because he could not see.

The wife began to cry.   The husband refused to go away without his wife.

They went to court and the blind man explained that he and his wife had been traveling on their donkey to Bitlis when the donkey became stubborn and would not move; this other man appeared and urged the donkey on and arrived with them in the city where he first tried to steal the donkey and then the wife.

The husband then told the truth, speaking bitterly and cursing himself for having such a soft heart.

The wife then told the truth and wept.

The Judge discovered that from the way the three spoke one could not tell which was lying, so he said, Place each of these in a separate room.   Let each be watched, and in the morning report to me what is learned.

This was done.

When the blind man thought he was alone he began to smile.   He then yawned, stretching his muscles.   He then began to dance.   He said to himself, I've got the donkey; if I can get the wife, mine will be the life.

The husband cursed himself over and over again for his stupidity in wanting to help a blind man.

The wife wept.

In the morning this information was given to the Judge.   He had the blind man placed in jail.   The husband and wife went away on their donkey.

VII

THERE WAS A blind man in a household to whom the others gave the best of all things: food, clothing, bed, covers, and all; yet he was filled with discontent and wailed all day and all night because of his ill-treatment. The family had water and gave the blind man milk; they had one cup of rice and gave him three; they had half a loaf of bread and gave him three loaves; but still he complained. In fury and despair the family killed a lamb, roasted it, placed it on a platter, and put it before the blind man. He smelled it, began touching it to find out how large it was, and then began to eat, but before he had swallowed the first bite he said, If this much comes to me, how much goes to you?

The Warm, Quiet Valley of Home

MY COUSIN DROVE the broken-down Ford to the front
of the house and pulled the emergency brake because the
regular brakes were no good. The car skidded, choked and
stopped. He got out and came around the house to the
back yard and stood a little while looking up at the sky.
Then he came up the steps and on into the kitchen.

I was almost through shaving.

It's going to be a swell day, he said.

That's fine, I said.

He poured himself a cup of coffee and sat down and
began to have breakfast. Bread and butter and coffee and
Armenian cheese and black olives.

I dried my face and poured coffee into the other cup
on the table and began to eat.

It was a big percolator. He drank four cups and I
drank three; I would have had four cups myself, only
there wasn't any more coffee in the percolator.

It was still dark when we left the house.

We've got a swell lunch, he said. I fixed it myself.

Anything to drink? I said.

Beer, he said. Six bottles. I've got them in a box with wet burlap on the bottom and top, so they won't get too hot.

Can't we get some ice? I said.

Well, sure, he said. But it'll melt.

That's all right, I said. We can drink the beer before we have lunch. It won't melt before ten in the morning, will it?

It gets pretty hot after daybreak, he said.

I don't like warm beer, I said.

I know where we can get some ice at this hour, he said.

Is it very far out of the way? I said.

No, he said.

I'll crank, I said.

No, he said. Let me crank. I know how to get this motor going.

He cranked, the motor started, we got in and drove away.

I don't suppose there are any streams up that way, I said.

There used to be a brook somewhere up there, he said. It might be dry this time of year, though.

Did you bring the guns? I said.

Hell yes, he said. If you hit anything with that twenty-two, it'll be luck, though.

Why? I said.

Something's the matter with the sight, he said.

Maybe it's your eye, I said.

I got a good eye, he said. It ain't my eye. I aimed at a cotton-tail not more than twenty yards away and missed.

It's probably your eye, I said.

How about the shot-gun?

It's O. K., he said.

Anything the matter with the sight? I said.

No, but you don't need the sight, he said.

Oh, I said.

The old Ford rattled down Ventura Avenue and then slowed down. My cousin pulled the emergency brake and the car skidded and stopped in front of a Coal & Ice place that had an office up front and a light on in the office. My cousin went up and tried the door, but it was locked. He looked through the window and saw a man sleeping in a chair, so he knocked at the door. After a while the man opened the door and said, What do you want?

Pennsylvania coal, my cousin said.

Ain't got no coal this time of year, the man said.

O. K., my cousin said, we'll take ice, then.

How much ice do you want? the man said.

Give me a dime's worth, my cousin said.

The man disappeared and came back half a minute later with a cube of ice in a canvas bag.

Got a pick? my cousin said.

Sure, the man said.

The man brought the ice to the car and my cousin took the ice out of the canvas bag and put it on the running board. Then he took the ice pick from the man and began chipping the cube and putting the pieces between the wet burlap around the bottles of beer.

My cousin gave the man a dime, and the man went back to his office and chair.

My cousin chipped the cube into small pieces and put all the pieces in the wet burlap; then he cranked the car and got in.

We turned north near the County Hospital. It began to be day. The sky was very fine and the hospital looked very sad.

Were you ever in a hospital? my cousin said.

Yes, I said.

What did you have? he said.

Nothing, I said. I was visiting.

Visiting who? he said.

Do you remember Kerop who died? I said. You weren't very old when he was around.

I remember, he said.

Well, I was visiting him, I said.

What did he have? my cousin said.

T. B., I said.

What sort of a guy was he, anyway? my cousin said.

He was O. K., I said. I used to take him grapes and figs and peaches. He wasn't very old when he died. He wasn't forty. I was ten or eleven.

When we reached Clovis the sun was up and the town was very pleasant-looking. My cousin drove around town four or five times, looking at the place.

Then my cousin pulled the emergency brake and the car stopped in front of a general merchandise store. There were no people in the town.

Do you want to walk around in this town? he said.

How about some more breakfast? I said.

Got any money? my cousin said.

About a dollar and twenty cents, I said.

All right, if we can find a place, he said.

We got out of the car and walked along the main street of the little town. There wasn't much to the town. It was just a lot of sad-looking wooden buildings facing a couple of sad-looking streets, a lot of sad-looking store windows, a lot of sad-looking doors and signs and second-story windows. And just beyond the town you could see the vineyards. It was just a little place in the country surrounded by vines, but it was very pleasant being there early in the morning.

My cousin went behind a shack that was empty and for rent.

Did I ever tell you about the colored boy who went up to the doctor? my cousin said.

No, I said.

That's a funny one, my cousin said. I like the jokes of this country more than the serious things. The serious things are funny too, but they're funny because they ain't supposed to be funny. Do you remember that guy who came to town and pitched a big tent and preached?

You mean that revivalist? I said. Sure I remember him.

He was all right, my cousin said. I didn't like the saw-dust on the floor and the wooden benches and the canvas roof. That didn't seem like a church. He was an earnest man, though. It was very funny when he prayed. I could hardly keep from busting out laughing. The people were a lot funnier than the preacher. They were scared to death.

We went back to the main street of the town and found a restaurant, only it was closed.

There wasn't a soul in town, even though the sun was up and it was beginning to be hot.

Shall we wait for this place to open up, my cousin said, or shall we go on and eat some of the lunch and drink a bottle of beer each in the country?

This place may not open up for hours yet, I said.

I don't know why they ever opened this place in the first place, my cousin said. I'd like to meet the guy who did it.

What sort of a guy do you think he'd be? he said.

I figure he'd be a sort of an amiable sort of a guy, I said.

I don't mean amiable, my cousin said. I mean what the hell do you figure made him go and open up a restaurant in a town like this?

Maybe he's got a big appetite, I said. Maybe he takes care of that.

I'll bet ten to one that's the answer, my cousin said. He's a little guy with a big appetite. He doesn't want to go hungry, *any time*. He wants to have stuff near by all the time. So he has the restaurant. If the worst comes to the worst, he can eat all the hash himself.

I think we've solved the whole problem, I said, so we don't need to wait.

We went back to the hack and my cousin cranked it and we drove out of the town.

The hills were brown and dry. The grass was all dead and dry. We traveled about ten miles and then it was the place my cousin said was fine. It was a good place. It was cool and very pleasant, although the weather was very hot. There were trees that had grown up by themselves, on the slopes of the hills, and beneath the trees was grass that wasn't dry. We ate three beef sandwiches each and drank a bottle of beer each, and then we took the guns and the rest of the lunch, except the beer, and began to walk.

We walked about an hour and didn't see anything to shoot, so my cousin shot at a white butterfly with the twenty-two and missed.

See? he said. Something's the matter with the sight.

Give me that gun, I said.

I shot at a butterfly and missed too.

Sounds all right, I said.

Sounds just like a twenty-two, my cousin said.

Where the hell's that brook? I said.

What brook? my cousin said.

What do you mean, what brook? I said. *The brook.* Didn't you speak of a brook this morning?

I don't think there's any water in it, my cousin said.

It ain't a brook unless there's water in it, I said.

All of a sudden my cousin fired the shot-gun and I saw a jack-rabbit jump and run.

Something's the matter with the sight on that shot-gun, I said.

No, my cousin said, on second thought I decided not to kill an innocent animal. After all, what good would it do me?

We walked two hours before we found the brook. There was a little water in it, but the water was stagnant and stank. Nevertheless, we sat down on the cool grass and talked.

My cousin wanted to know some more about the man who died in the County Hospital. Kerop, our third uncle. I told him, and then he told me about a boy who drowned in Thompson Ditch. A friend of his named Harlan Beach.

He was a good guy, my cousin said.

It was very quiet and pleasant. I laid flat on my back and looked up at the sky. A lot of crazy years had gone by all right. A lot of crazy things had happened all right. It was September again and it was very pleasant. It was very hot, but it was very pleasant too. This was my valley, where I had been born. This earth and sky was home. This temperature was. My cousin was. The way he talked was. The memories he knew were part of it. The people he remembered. I looked up at the sky and remembered New York. I had lived there less than a year ago, when I was twenty years old, but it seemed as if it were *ten* years ago, or twenty, or a hundred. And it seemed as if I had never lived there, or had only dreamed of having lived there, a long summer and winter dream of sultriness and stickiness and crazy buildings and crazy crowds and crazy subways, and then bitter cold, snow and wind, and the black sunless sky.

My cousin talked in English, and I talked partly in English and partly in Armenian. Then he began to talk partly in English and partly in Armenian, and after a while we talked in Armenian only.

Poor Kerop, my cousin said. Poor, poor, poor. He used to walk; now he does not walk.

My cousin moved the palms of his hands together which is the Armenian symbol of the ending of a thing.

Let us eat bread, I said.

Let us eat bread and remember, my cousin said.

We ate all the sandwiches.

Then we started walking back to the car so we could drink the beer.

There were no animals or birds to shoot along the way. There were a number of small singing birds, but we did not shoot at them.

Let us salute the absent inhabitants of the world, my cousin said.

That's a noble thought, I said.

We lifted the guns to our shoulders and pointed them at nothing in the sky.

To the dead, my cousin said.

We fired the guns.

The sound was half-crazy and half-tragic.

To Kerop, I said.

We fired again.

To Harlan Beach, my cousin said, and again we fired.

To everybody who once lived on this earth and died, my cousin said.

We fired the guns.

The shot-gun made ten times as much noise as the twenty-two.

Give me the shot-gun for this next one, I said.

My cousin gave me the shot-gun and I gave him the twenty-two.

Who will it be? he said.

To my father, I said. I squeezed the trigger of the shot-gun. It had a powerful kick.

To *my* father, my cousin said.

We fired again.

To my grandfather, I said.

To *my* grandfather, my cousin said.

To Gregory the Illuminator, I said.

To Bedros Tourian, my cousin said.

To Raffi, I said.

We would walk a little way and stop and name someone who was dead, and fire the guns.

To Antranik, my cousin said.

To Khetcho, I said.

Poor Khetcho, my cousin said in Armenian.

To Mourad, I said.

We saluted many Armenian soldiers and scholars and writers and priests. We saluted many great men who were dead.

We made a lot of noise in the hills, but it was all right because there was nobody around.

When we got back to the car the beer was not quite as cold as it had been in the morning, but it was cool and good to drink.

We drank the beer, my cousin cranked the car, we got in and drove out of the hills into the warm, quiet, lovely valley that was our home in the world.

A Number of the Poor

ONE SUMMER I worked two months in a grocery store. I worked from four in the afternoon till midnight, but after eight o'clock there wouldn't be any business to speak of and all I'd do was look out the window or go around the store and keep things in order. It was a little store on Grove Street, in the slums. The people who came to the store were all interesting and poor.

Only two or three of them didn't steal things, not counting little children. Almost all the others stole more than they bought. It was just that they needed the stuff and didn't have enough money to buy it. They'd put a package of chewing gum in a pocket when my back was turned, or a small cake, or a can of tomato soup. I knew all about it, but I never let on. They were all good people, just poor.

Once in August a lady tried to hide a cantaloupe in her waist. That was one of the saddest things I ever saw. She was a woman of fifty or so. It was obvious that she had a lot more under her waist than herself and I guess she just had to have a cantaloupe. That evening she didn't buy anything. I guess she was broke. She spent about five minutes in the store, asking about the prices of a lot of things, and tasting apricots and peaches and figs. I'd tell her figs were ten cents a dozen and very good and she'd say they looked good but were they really? Then I'd tell her to taste one. She'd hesitate a little and then lift a very big one out of the crate, peel it and very thoughtfully swallow it in three bites, tasting it carefully. She was always a lady. With a little money to go with her charm I believe she would have cut an impressive figure in a grocery store, but she never seemed to have any. I thought it was wonderful the way she got the cantaloupe without losing her dignity.

One of the few who came to the store and never stole anything was a little Spaniard named Casal. You had to know which stole and which didn't. Casal was one of those small men with big heads and sad faces that you notice right away and wonder about. He used to come to the store almost every night at ten and stay for a half hour or so to talk. He was quiet-spoken and solemn and dignified. If you're no bigger than a boy of eleven, and weigh about ninety-two pounds, it's no cinch to be dignified.

I always had a lot of respect for Casal. He didn't seem to know anything. I don't suppose he'd read a newspaper in ten years. He had no ideas and no complaints about anything. He was just a very small man who had managed to stay alive forty-eight years. Little by little I came to know why he was so dignified and had no need to complain about anything.

It was because he was a father. He had a son of sixteen. This boy was six feet tall and very handsome. He was Casal's boy all right; there was no getting around that. He had his father's head. Casal was very proud of him; that's what kept him going. One evening he said: You know my boy? He is a fine boy. So big and good. Do you know what? Every night when I come home from work my boy says, Pa, get on my shoulders. I get on his shoulders and he carries me all around the house. Then we sit down and eat.

What can you make of something like that? That small father and that great son, the boy carrying the father around on his shoulders? There's something there, I think.

Another night Casal said, I'll tell you why my boy is such a good boy. His mother died when he was born. That's the reason. He never knew his mother. He was always alone. Even when he was a baby. I used to go home in my lunch hour to see how he was. Sometimes he'd be crying. Sometimes he'd be through crying and he'd be all alone waiting. He stopped crying when he was just a little baby. He learned to know how it was. After he was two years old it was a lot easier for him and for me too. You should have seen the way he grew. Do you like him?

I think he's a fine boy, I said.

Well, I'll tell you, Casal said. Do you know what? He wants me to stop working. He wants to work for me now. He says I've worked enough. He's good with machines. He can get a job as a mechanic in a repair shop. You know what I told him? I told him no. I told him, Joe, you're going to college. He gets along fine everywhere.

He's a good boy. I'm going to send him through college.
He's got a right. I like to work for him.

Sure, I said.

Casal was one of the fine ones who came to that store
when I worked there.

There was a little red-head, about twelve, who was
another. Her name was Maggie. She was very powerful,
the way some kids of the poor are, and full of the swellest
laughter in the world.

She used to come into the store and bust out laughing,
right out of a clear sky, no preliminaries, no explanations
or anything. She'd just come in and laugh. That always
pleased me, but I'd never let her know it. So she'd laugh
some more.

All right, I'd say. What do you want?

You know, she'd say.

Laughter.

A loaf of bread?

Bread! she'd say.

Well, what *do* you want?

Out of the corner of her eye, a glance.

What have you got?

There wouldn't be anything else to do with somebody
like that, so I'd toss her a peach which she would catch and
eat very daintily. Spoofing, though, of course, with her
little finger extended.

They say I look like Ginger Rogers, she'd say.

They're liars.

I do, she'd say. You know I do. Do you like her?

She's swell, I'd say.

I look just like her, she'd say.

Twelve years old.

The country's full of them too, and it's no use worrying about them. They're all in the big movie.

Another was the little boy who never had a penny but always came to look. About four years old. I used to call him Callaghan. He was great. He'd spend an hour looking at the penny candies and never say a word, except maybe to himself. People would stumble over him but he'd stick to his spot and keep looking.

One evening the lady who stole the cantaloupe patted him on the head.

Your son? she said.

Yes, I said.

A fine boy, she said. He resembles you. How much are figs today?

Ten cents a dozen, I said.

Are they really good?

Yes, they are. I ate one five minutes ago. Please try one.

She did; and tried also a peach and an apricot.

She didn't buy anything that night either. She stayed ten minutes and I know she wanted to ask if she might borrow twenty-five cents till tomorrow, but didn't dare. At last she said, We're lucky to be living in California, aren't we?

I've never been out of the state, I said. I've never been out of this city. Is it different in other places?

Oh terribly, she said. Why, there are places you can hardly breathe in in the summertime. Chicago. And look how wonderful it is here.

She was at the open door and waved her arm gently outward at the sky.

The *air* is so fine here, she said.

When she was gone I called Callaghan. He came over immediately.

Would you like a licorice strap?

No answer.

He would, of course, but he wouldn't say so.

Come over here and take what you like, I said.

He came over behind the candy case but didn't reach to take anything.

Take anything you like, I said.

He looked at me, a little uncertain.

Sure, I said. You can have anything you like.

He couldn't believe it and was a little scared.

It's all right, I said.

He reached out and took a licorice strap.

Take something else, I said.

He put back the licorice strap and reached for a wax dog.

No, I said. Keep the licorice strap, too.

In all he took four different kinds of penny candies, but it took a lot of encouragement from me to get him to do it.

Okay, Callaghan, I said. Now go home and eat them. Take them with you.

Without a word, but still amazed, he went away.

The next day when he came back he said very quietly, The best is the licorice strap.

In that case, I said, I'll try one myself.

So I got him one and one for myself and together we ate them.

It was a good job while it lasted because of the fine, funny, tragic, little poor people who came there for things to eat or somebody to talk to.

The Monumental Arena

At THE WATERFRONT they told me about the trouble. They put the blame on one head and then on another. The men were sullen.

There was one who had been clubbed. He was a sad-faced Scandinavian. What this boy said I could understand.

He said it was a thing he could not speak about to the others because they had one idea in mind, and he had several. They were good men, he said, but he was a man who could read a book and stand up and go to work and, working, remember what he had read. Every word, he said.

They had clubbed him and he was without hate. He even laughed, saying it was funny. The man who clubbed him, doing it with hate. He said he saw the man, a police. The man was frightened. He felt sorry for the man. And then the club came down on his head and he laughed out loud and became unconscious.

When he awoke, he was in the smell of the emergency hospital. Six others were there, one a woman. He felt all the ugliness and lost his temper because the woman, who was really hurt, was swearing and crying and saying she could kill every cop on the waterfront.

He got up, he said, feeling angry, and was about to lift the table from the floor and smash it against the wall, because it was too much to hear the woman swearing and crying, and then he remembered how funny it was, and sat down.

The young doctor asked if he was all right. He told the young doctor he was all right all right, only if he didn't have a little drink he might get sore, and he didn't want to. The doctor told him sure. He swallowed the drink and began to smile, the woman still crying. Now it was as bad as before and he knew it, only he was accepting it differently, because of the drink. It was a lie, but he said what of it? Since it was *all* a lie? It was better to smile. He felt sorry for the young doctor. For the man who had clubbed him he felt *bitterly* sorry, because he knew the man was a coward when he might not be.

He talked quietly, saying it was not easy for him to listen to the woman crying. He told the young doctor he was going away. He wrote his name in the book and told the doctor he had no address because he had no money and would not stay in a free place. He said the doctor did not like it, and began to swear. The doctor gave the Scandinavian a dollar and the Scandinavian accepted the dollar, because it was different. It was the way the doctor swore that made it different. It wasn't a shame. The doctor was a young man who had gone through college and learned about curing the body of pains, and the way he swore made the acceptance possible.

It was a thing to remember, to place against the lifted club of the police and the insanity of the weeping woman.

He walked down the steps of the emergency hospital, smiling, because it was true. There was and could be one of one kind as much as one of another. The swearing of the doctor proved it: angry kindliness or angry hate, decency in man or the other thing.

At the waterfront I listened to the young Scandinavian. At the same time the others talked, I could understand the significance of the talk without understanding the words, because the words were only the outward form of the thing, which is not important, and the talking was the thing itself. But I could understand the significance *and* the words when the Scandinavian talked because they were one and the same.

The strong body has a wisdom beyond language, but if you are clubbed and your equilibrium is destroyed and you fall, laughing, and waken in the smell of a hospital, and hear weeping, and feel sudden insanity, and learn of decency in man, the body is apt, if you have read two or three books by good men, to find articulation and to utter timeless belief and faith, its humility and its pious anger, and this boy spoke without effort, speaking for himself.

He said he was sorry for everybody because when he was clubbed and while he was laughing and while he was falling and his balance was being taken from his body and mind and he could not determine who or what to hate or love there occurred in him only one thing, white, like snow, quiet, like weeping music, and this thing was *pity*. It was pity for the man who had struck him and pity for all the others on strike, for the rich who were using the police and the clubs of the police, and for all rich and all poor in all cities and in all countries, for man everywhere, caught in the monumental arena, helplessly the victim of a vicious and stupid game, wanting something, wanting a breath of free and pure air, escape, to go beyond the walls of the arena, to stand alive and whole. He said he saw life caught in the small arena as he fell. The air there, he said, was stifling. He could feel life suffocating, and he did not know what happened finally, except that he remembered nations of them running against the wall of the monumental arena, and that was all.

When he awoke in the hospital he could almost remember what happened after, but he could not quite do it, and all that he remembered was *their* running and *his* pity. Then he heard the woman weeping and swearing, and he wanted to destroy the whole place.

He said he could not understand.

We want something, he said, but we do not know what. It is all in the books, our wanting, but we do not know what.

He looked at the others who were talking, and smiled.

They think they want more money, he said, but that isn't all.   Better working hours, he said, but that isn't all either. It is something beyond these. More, he said. More and beyond. It is in all the books, not in the writing, but it is there. And many died, he said, wanting. Something we have lost perhaps, he said. We cannot remember what it is but sometimes, sometimes in sleep, we remember that it is lost, and when we get up in the morning we think it is money we want, but that isn't all. The rich are sometimes more miserable than the poor, and they have enough money to buy everything that can be bought. There is a mistake in some place of our life.

He took the dollar from his pocket and smiled at it. It was the gift of the young doctor.

I have had it two days and I am never going to spend it, he said. When I left the hospital, he said, I needed a drink badly and I went to The Palace Bar. Then something happened and I would not spend the money. It was the way the doctor swore, wanting to help me and help everybody, and if I used the money it would destroy the feeling I had of gratitude. I am keeping it, he said. Either, he said, for giving to another when the time comes, or for giving back to the doctor. It is money, he said, if I spend it. If I do not spend it, he said, it is many things, maybe what we have lost and are trying to get back.

Peace, It's Wonderful

THE JUDGE SAID he was sorry but the young man was guilty of hopping.

Two eager, middle-aged, slum-dwelling, white women with memories got up in the first row and said, Thank you, Father. Peace, it's wonderful.

The Judge ducked, called for order, and said, Never mind that Father stuff. You ladies are old enough to be my mother. I will now pronounce sentence.

The sentence was five years in the Federal Penitentiary.

That ought to hold him a while, the Judge thought.

The young man told reporters he was happy and at peace with the world. He said powerful vibrations had been coming to him from New York. He said he was exhausted and looked forward to spending the next five years in holy seclusion. He told the reporters he had been wanting to write a book, and now he was going to have his chance.

Thank you, Father, he said. Peace, it's wonderful.

The Judge was disgusted.

It ain't right, somebody said. A good honest religious

young man like that with nothing but love in his bones don't deserve punishment like that.

What is dis stuff? Manuel the pool shark said. Everywhere I go everybody saying Peace.

We went around the corner to Pete's and had two beers and a steak sandwich each. Then we went across the street to the North Beach Branch of that religious order. In the window was a picture of the man and beneath the picture was the opinion that the man was God.

It was eleven o'clock at night. Two American girls of the half-wit school came out of the place and stood on the porch. Behind them was a large good-natured Negro woman who might have been a maid in any one of the whorehouses in that neighborhood. There was a bunch of bananas in the room, as well as a shelf of canned goods, mostly beans.

O.K., Sport, Manuel said. Flash de smile. Give out de personality.

These girls? I said.

Sure, Manuel said.

Good evening, I said to the Negro woman. How much are the bananas?

Thank you, Father, she said.

The two girls said, Peace, it's wonderful.

Oh boy, Manuel said.

Bananas are thirty cents a dozen, the Negro woman said. Peace.

I'll take a dozen and a half, I said. Thank you.

We went into the hall. The girls moved to go. Manuel

said, Amen, and gave the girls the religious eye. They smiled piously and vibrated.

I helped the Negro woman count out a dozen and a half bananas. When I turned around Manuel was gone. I saw him at the corner with a girl on each arm.

He turned around and hollered, Hurry up, Joe. Peace, it's wonderful.

I went back to Pete's and gave the bananas to a Chinese newsboy.

Manuel showed up a little before two in the morning. Peace, I said.

It was all lousy, he said. What is dis stuff?

Piano

I GET EXCITED EVERY time I see a piano, Ben said.

Is that so? Emma said. Why?

I don't know, Ben said. Do you mind if we go into this store and try the little one in the corner?

Can you play? Emma said.

If you call what I do playing, Ben said.

What do you do?

You'll see, Ben said.

They went into the store, to the small piano in the corner. Emma noticed him smiling and wondered if she'd ever know anything about him. She'd go along for a while thinking she knew him and then all of a sudden she'd know she didn't. He stood over the piano, looking down at it. What she imagined was that he had probably heard good piano playing and loved that kind of music and every time he saw a keyboard and the shape of a piano he remembered the music and imagined he had something to do with it.

Can you play? she said.

Ben looked around. The clerks seemed to be busy.

I can't play, Ben said.

She saw his hands go quietly to the white and black keys, like a real pianist's, and it seemed very unusual because of what she felt when that happened. She felt that he was someone who would be a long time finding out about himself, and someone somebody else would be much longer finding out about. He should be somebody who could play a piano.

Ben made a few quiet chords. Nobody came over to try to sell him anything, so, still standing, he began to do what he'd told her wasn't playing.

Well, all she knew was that it was wonderful.

He played half a minute only. Then he looked at her and said, It sounds good.

I think it's wonderful, Emma said.

I don't mean what *I* did, Ben said. I mean the piano. I mean the piano itself. It has a fine tone, especially for a little piano.

A middle-aged clerk came over and said, How do you do?

Hello, Ben said. This is a swell one.

It's a very popular instrument, the clerk said. Especially fine for apartments. We sell a good many of them.

How much is it? Ben said.

Two hundred forty-nine fifty, the clerk said. You can have terms, of course.

Where do they make them? Ben said.

I'm not sure, the clerk said. In Philadelphia, I think. I can find out.

Don't bother, Ben said. Do you play?

No, I don't, the clerk said.

He noticed Ben wanting to try it out some more.

Go ahead, he said. Try it some more.

I don't play, Ben said.

I heard you, the clerk said.

That's not playing, Ben said. I can't read a note.

Sounded good to me, the clerk said.

Me, too, Emma said. How much is the first payment?

Oh, the clerk said. Forty or fifty dollars. Go ahead, he said, I'd like to hear you play some more.

If this was the right kind of room, Ben said, I could sit down at the piano for hours.

Play some more, the clerk said. Nobody'll mind.

The clerk pushed up the bench and Ben sat down and began to do what he said wasn't playing. He fooled around fifteen or twenty seconds and then found something like a melody and stayed with it two minutes. Before he was through the music became quiet and sorrowful and Ben himself became more and more pleased with the piano. While he was letting the melody grow, he talked to the clerk about the piano. Then he stopped playing and stood up.

Thanks, he said. Wish I could buy it.

Don't mention it, the clerk said.

Ben and Emma walked out of the store. In the street Emma said, I didn't know about that, Ben.

About what? Ben said.

About you.

What about me?

Being that way, Emma said.

This is my lunch hour, Ben said. In the evening is when I like to think of having a piano.

They went into a little restaurant and sat at the counter and ordered sandwiches and coffee.

Where did you learn to play? Emma said.

I've never learned, Ben said. Any place I find a piano, I try it out. I've been doing that ever since I was a kid. Not having money does that.

He looked at her and smiled. He smiled the way he did when he stood over the piano looking down at the keyboard. Emma felt very flattered.

Never having money, Ben said, keeps a man away from lots of things he figures he ought to have by rights.

I guess it does, Emma said.

In a way, Ben said, it's a good thing, and then again it's not so good. In fact, it's terrible.

He looked at her again, the same way, and she smiled back at him the way he was smiling at her.

She understood. It was like the piano. He could stay near it for hours. She felt very flattered.

They left the restaurant and walked two blocks to The Emporium where she worked.

Well, so long, he said.

So long, Ben, Emma said.

He went on down the street and she went on into the store. Somehow or other she knew he'd get a piano some day, and everything else, too.

The Mouse

He was a little man with a sad look in his eye; an uncertain posture, as if he were held together only temporarily and might at any moment break into all sorts of ridiculous, surrealist fragments. He was not nervous as very strong people sometimes are. He was on edge, but friendly. That was because he was afraid; a mouse among many cats. He was hungry and so were the cats, so he was friendly and good-natured.

He called them all killers.

Hi-ya, Killer, he would say to Sam. Sam wouldn't even look at him. Look, Killer, he'd say to Dopey, I got a horse in this next race that's a cinch. He'd try to smile and seem one of the cats, but Dopey would give him a dirty look and say, All right, Mouse, you've got a horse in the next race that's a cinch, so bet him to win, or ride him, or eat him. You're hungry, so eat the horse.

Ha ha, Mouse would say, I could eat a horse at that.

Sam himself, though, and Dopey too, were no better than Mouse. They just happened to be less temporarily held together. They just happened to be able to take it better than the little fellow. If no one talked to them they didn't feel lonely and scared. If they didn't eat they didn't suffer the way he suffered. If they gambled and lost they didn't feel like falling down somewhere and dying.

In a way they were his inferiors. He was at least critical of the world. He only wanted to be one of them, the ones who were no good in the world. He didn't want to be making up to the world any more because he knew it was no use. He'd tried long enough to get by as a clerk or something in some corner of the world, some corner of commerce or industry or something. There was no place for him out there, so he wasn't eager to go out any more and try to make a place for himself. He talked about it a good deal whenever he found somebody who would listen and he swore a good deal, spitting at every opportunity, being one of the boys, turning around suddenly to see if anybody was going to play a joke on him again. He'd always laugh, and try to be one of the gang. Blackie or somebody else big would lift him off the floor by the seat of his pants and trot him out of the place and drop him in the alley and he would stand in the alley a moment, trying to decide what to do, and after a while he'd come back in, talking at the top of his voice while everybody roared with laughter.

The others of course were stupid, not strong. They didn't understand that in a way he was the best of them, the gamest, and the one who was having the most trouble and taking it better than anybody else. They didn't realize that when they were unfriendly to him they were behaving like the smug ones in the world, the ones who had kicked *them* out and told them to stay out. They were enjoying a vicious and wretched kind of superiority. He was a little brother and instead of being kind to him they hurt him all the time and wouldn't even do him the favor of letting him be useful to them once in a while. He was always eager to be helpful to any of them. He was always the first to offer to go on an errand, but they always pushed him out of the way and sent somebody else. They didn't even want him to feel useful. He took it all and showed up every day and stayed until the races were over, and even though he never seemed to have a nickel to his name he managed better than the others to keep from coughing.

One day a big lout named Harry won eighteen dollars on a race and felt so superior that he began to pick on the little fellow.

What do you eat, Mouse? he said. Where do you sleep?

The little fellow was scared to death because of the money Harry had in his pocket and didn't know what to say.

If Harry hadn't won all the money he would have said, I eat the same things you eat, and I sleep where you do, in empty stores. But now he didn't know what to say. It wasn't easy for him to lie. He stood uneasily, fidgeting, trying to think of a good answer and then he said:

I eat Irish stew and sleep in a bed.

This was too desperate a reply not to be funny and everybody busted out laughing. Everybody knew that what the Mouse was saying was that he wished to God he could eat Irish stew and sleep in a bed for a change.

Then Harry asked a question that made everybody laugh.

Somebody goosed the little fellow. He jumped and tried to get into a corner while everybody crowded around him, pretending to want to touch him, making him shrink and bend and put his hands in front of him and then in back. When he was safe in the corner everybody waited for him to talk. Everybody was all primed to bust out laughing no matter what he said. He looked about fearfully and when he spoke his voice cracked.

I've got a girl, he said.

The laughter was hysterical. Everybody went around shoving and striking one another, saying, He's got a girl.

One of them who wasn't much bigger than Mouse himself and a good deal more of a weakling tried to embrace the little fellow. The little one pushed the other in the face. It was all an accident. He just didn't want anybody with a face like that to kiss him. The other one stopped being funny and smashed a hard fist into the little one's face and the little one crumpled into the corner and sat down. His eye began to swell and his lips were trembling and before Harry lifted the other one off the floor and ran him out into the alley, the Mouse, almost crying, said, Well, I have. I can show you her picture.

Everybody was a little disgusted with the whole episode now, and Harry pushed through everybody and took care of the other little guy who knocked the Mouse down.

Who the hell are you? Harry said. This was my joke.

He ran the other fellow out into the alley, and the other fellow never came back to the place again. The next day, though, the little one was there the same as ever. That made everybody have a little respect for him. His left eye was badly swollen, but at least he was there. He was very quiet of course, but so was everybody else.

Harry was the richest one in the dump for three days. Then he had his normal run of bad luck and once again he was broke. He went on being broke for four days, and it looked like he was going to be broke for a long time to come. One day, just before post time on the last race, the little fellow, who was standing beside Harry, said quietly, I really *have* got a girl. Do you want to see her picture?

No, Harry said. I believe you. *I* haven't got a girl and neither have any of these other lugs.

The Adventures of a Young Man Some Day to Be Another Jack London

Wʜᴇɴ ʏᴏᴜ ɢᴏ ᴀᴡᴀʏ from home the first time in your life you're usually a year or two under twenty. You're usually ambitious and anxious to be a newspaperman or something. You're usually eager to meet exciting people and do wonderful things. That's how it was with Joe two years ago when he left my home town and came to Frisco, the same as me ten years ago.

He was a boy people looked at twice in the hope of finding out if he was just dumb or got that expression from having one great idea after another. He was a little under six feet, broad-shouldered, good-looking one minute and ordinary-looking the next. It all depended on when you happened to look at him.

He'd had a year at State College: football, public speaking, and the leading role in the college production of *Emperor Jones*.

He wrote for the college magazine, too. It was a story called *A Guy With a Good Heart*, and of course it was about himself. It was about how he gave a bum

in the street who'd taken him for somebody with money
his last quarter because he didn't want to disappoint the
bum. The best thing about the story was that it didn't
say the bum didn't need the quarter.

That's how I knew Joe had a good heart or a poor
imagination.

It turned out that his imagination was all right. As
for his heart, it was one of the best that ever got broken.

When he came to Frisco he didn't get in touch with
me for a month. He arrived in town with thirty-seven
dollars, and didn't have a job when the money gave out.
He walked through town one whole night because he
didn't have any money for a room. The next day he came
up to see me, but not to borrow money. He wanted to
borrow my typewriter. He wanted to write a story. He
wanted to write about what he'd seen while walking
through town all night.

What *did* you see? I asked him.

Believe me, he said. Nothing. That's what I want to
write about. If I had money, I wouldn't be that way.

No? I said. Let me lend you some money till you get
started.

Thanks, he said. All I want is a typewriter.

All right, I said. You can have a typewriter, but suppose you *do* write the story, suppose it *is* great, what then?

What then? he said. It'll be written, that's all.

Let's go get some breakfast, I said.

Supper for me, he said.

All right, I said. I've had breakfast. I'll have lunch.

You have supper. We'll manage somehow. We'll explain the whole thing to the waitress.

What waitress? Joe said.

Any waitress, I said.

Oh, he said. I thought maybe you knew a waitress.

I know a couple of waitresses, I said. I know them only by their first names of course, but if necessary I can ask them their last names.

No, he said. I thought you knew somebody you wanted me to meet. I hope to marry and settle down some day, you know.

You've got to have a waitress of course, I said.

No, he said. You're getting everything wrong. I'll marry the first waitress we happen to run into if she can sing and is beautiful and likes me.

How many meals have you missed so far? I said.

Three or four, Joe said.

Are you running a fever or anything?

No. Why?

Well, if you've missed three or four meals and aren't running a fever and talk the way you do, you're a natural-born writer.

It's the truth, Joe said. But do you think Scoop Healy cares about that?

Who's Scoop Healy?

He's the best city editor in San Francisco.

How do you know?

He said so himself.

He did? How did that happen?

I told him he didn't know his business. Then he told me he was the best city editor in San Francisco and if I didn't believe him I could go to hell or ask any newspaperman in town. He said I could go to hell anyway.

What did you say?

Well, Joe said, what *could* I say. I told him I was sorry. I told him I hadn't known he was the best city editor in San Francisco.

What did he say to that?

He said to go to hell.

Why?

Because he was ten minutes behind deadline.

I sat down again. So did Joe—for two seconds.

Ten minutes behind deadline? I said. How'd you happen to run into him at a time like that? City editors don't interview applicants for jobs at a time like that.

Friend of mine got me into the editorial room at six in the morning, Joe said. I hid under a desk until I saw his shoes.

Scoop's shoes?

Yes. Friend of mine told me they were big brown oxfords.

Who is this friend of yours? I said.

The telephone operator, Joe said.

What telephone operator?

The one that works from midnight till eight in the morning at *The News*. Alice.

Oh, I said. Alice.

What did you do when you saw his shoes?

Well, Joe said, I said, Pardon me, Mr. Healy, can I have a moment of your time?

Don't tell me you were hiding under *his* desk?

Of course, Joe said. I didn't want an interview with the re-write man.

Go on, I said. I know you're hungry, but let's get this straight before we eat. If we don't, the food will be poison.

So I asked him if I could have a moment of his time.

What did the best city editor in San Francisco say to that? In view of your addressing him from underneath his desk?

He said no.

What?

That's right, Joe said. He said no.

Joe, I said, you're sure you're not running a fever from not having had three or four important meals? Three or four meals are pretty important to a growing boy, you know.

Growing boy? Joe said. I'm nineteen. And a good writer, too.

I know, I said. If I'm not badly mistaken, you're going to be another Mark Twain or somebody.

Jack London most likely, Joe said.

Jack London? I said.

Sure, Joe said.

Sure what? I said.

Sure, Mr. Harley, Joe said.

No, no, I said. I didn't mean for you to get formal. You don't need to call me Mr. Harley. I've known you since you were born in the house across the street from the house I was born in. What about Jack London?

I mean, Joe said, if you're not badly mistaken, I'm going to be another Jack London.

Why Jack London? I said. Instead of somebody else, I mean? You're not exactly the rugged out-door type.

I'm pretty rugged, Joe said. It's true I haven't been getting out-of-doors a great deal lately. But I'm more or less elemental about most things.

If you mean, I said, that when you haven't had three or four meals you get hungry.

No, Joe said. I mean about more things than getting hungry. Would you believe me if I told you I weigh one hundred and ninety pounds?

Yes, I would. Tell me.

I weigh one hundred and eighty-six pounds, Joe said.

Now more than ever I believe you. So you weigh one hundred and eighty-six pounds. So what?

Not one ounce of it's fat.

So what?

Well, Joe said, add two to two together and draw your own conclusion.

You mean you're *very* hungry? I said. *Very, very* hungry?

No, Joe said. I'm hungry all right, but that's not what I mean. I mean a guy like me has to have a girl.

A guy like you certainly does, I said.

I should say so, Joe said.

Well, now that we've got that settled, I said, let's go

back to the telephone operator who works from midnight till eight in the morning at *The News,* and the best city editor in San Francisco, Scoop Healy. After you've told me everything and had a bite to eat, you can come back here and write that story you want to write.

Thanks, Joe said. How are things going, Mr. Harley?

Not bad, I said. What did you do when Scoop Healy told you you couldn't have a moment of his time?

For a minute, Joe said, I just sat there. I hadn't counted on his saying I couldn't have a moment of his time, so I just sat there and tried to figure out what I ought to do next.

What did you decide?

Nothing. I didn't have time enough to figure out anything *brilliant.*

No? Why not?

All of a sudden Scoop Healy realized where I was. Under his desk, I mean. He jumped out of his chair and moved back and bent down to look at me.

Who are *you?* he said.

Joe Morgan, I said.

What are you doing under my desk? he said.

At the moment, I said, I'm sitting.

He started getting sore. I could tell he was getting sore from the way he was trying to be polite.

I see, I said. Go ahead.

Well, Joe said, he asked me what I wanted.

I want a job, I said.

We don't need a copy boy, he said.

Copy boy? I said. Mr. Healy, I'm one of the best newspapermen your paper is ever going to have on its staff. I'm on my way to New York.

How did he take that? I said.

Not very pleasantly, Joe said.

How could you tell?

Well, Joe said, from what he said. He told me to get the hell out from under his desk and hurry to New York.

What did you do? I said.

I got out from under his desk, Joe said, and offered to meet him more formally. I mean, I put out my hand. He took my hand and put his arm around me and I thought I had misjudged him when I believed him to be unfriendly, but I was right. I mean I was wrong when I thought I had misjudged him. I hadn't. I was right when I believed him to be unfriendly. With his arm around me he tried to *force* me toward the door.

Here Joe smiled as he did whenever he was remembering an episode in which everyone but himself had behaved stupidly.

And you know how many pounds I weigh, Joe said.

Yes, I said, you told me. I suppose your weight was no small thing to move toward the door.

Mr. Healy weighs at least two hundred pounds himself, Joe said.

Don't tell me you two had trouble, I said.

It wasn't my fault, Joe said.

Of course not, I said.

I wasn't the one who did the *first* pushing, Joe said.

Did you do some of the later pushing? I said.

A little, Joe said. We were talking all the time of course. He got more and more unfriendly and finally we started to wrestle. It wasn't my fault. I didn't mean to disarrange his clothes. As for his coat, he tore it himself. Then Miss Corbett told me to get off of Mr. Healy that very minute.

Miss Corbett? I said. Who's she?

Alice, Joe said. You know. The telephone operator.

Oh, I said. Did you get up?

Of course, Joe said. Mr. Healy got off the floor and bawled everybody out. They all went back to their desks.

Miss Corbett, he said, do you know this young gorilla?

He's no more a gorilla than you are, Miss Corbett said.

How did he get in here? Mr. Healy said. And what are you doing here at ten in the morning? You're off duty at eight.

She was waiting to find out how I would make out. Why?

Well, Joe said, I'd bet her two dollars I'd get a job.

I see, I said. You lost of course.

Not exactly, Joe said.

Not exactly? I said. Don't tell me he *hired* you.

No, Joe said. He didn't hire me, but he *may* hire me some day. I made a profound impression on his subconscious mind.

I should say you did, I said. Sticking your head out from under his desk the first thing in the morning. Asking him for a job. Bragging. Then wrestling him.

Thanks, Joe said. I'm hungry, but most of all I'm excited about this story I want to write.

All right, I said. Let's go get supper for you and lunch for me. After lunch for me and supper for you we'll come back here and you can go into the next room and close the door and write your story. I'm eager to see what it will be like.

Thanks, Mr. Harley, Joe said. It's not often a young man like me happens to get born in a house across the street from the house a man like you was born in.

I should say not.

We went out into the hall, talking, got into the elevator, talking, walked two blocks to Terry's, talking, took a booth, and went on talking.

It was the pleasantest thing I'd run into since I'd left Kingsburg myself. Joe had brought a lot of the old home town with him to the city. It was amusing to remember the place and the old years through the way he talked and smiled and got into every kind of trouble any young man from a small town ever got into in a big city, being ambitious and wanting to be a newspaperman and wanting to meet exciting people and have adventure and reach New York and be famous and fall in love and so on. It was pleasant to know the old home town was still making them that way.

Joe's supper was two orders of ham and eggs, five cups of coffee, and peach pie à la mode.

How do you like San Francisco? I said.

Fine, he said, but I got homesick last night.

We went back to my office. Griffis had fixed up the room I use for reading and loafing and taking naps. He'd cleared the desk and put a brand new rented typewriter and a bundle of white paper on it. When we got back to the office I opened the door of the room and told Joe to sit down and do his stuff.

Thanks very much, Mr. Harley, he said.

If you want anything, I said, just buzz. Mr. Griffis will be glad to get you anything, won't you, Mr. Griffis?

I certainly will, Griffis said.

I won't be wanting anything more, Joe said. Typewriter. Paper. Private office. That's all a writer needs.

He went into the office, closed the door, and two minutes later Griffis and I heard him pounding on the typewriter.

Extraordinary young man, Griffis said.

I saw him grow up, I said.

Little by little the typing slowed down, then stopped. An hour later Griffis opened the door of the room and found Joe asleep on the couch.

He was still asleep at six, so Griffis and I decided to let him go on sleeping. He had a troubled, child-like, sorrowful, yet amused expression on his face. I left five ten-dollar bills on the desk with a note.

Dear Joe:

When you wake up, here's a little money.

I glanced at the sheet of paper in the typewriter and read: *Now is the time for all good men to come to the aid of their party. Scoop Healy. Some day you'll remember me. Now is the time——*

Griffis and I tiptoed out of the room, closed the door, and left for the day.

In the morning Griffis found a typed short story on Joe's desk and a note for me.

Dear Mr. Harley: Joe wrote.

I'm sorry I fell asleep. I guess I was tired. You've been very kind. I'm borrowing the fifty dollars, but as I have nothing else I'm leaving as security this short story which I wrote when I woke up at ten minutes to eleven tonight. It is now three o'clock in the morning. Please take good care of the story for me until I pay you back the fifty dollars. Your friend and admirer,

Joe Morgan.

Joe called the story *A Night of Empty Streets*. It was about walking around town all night and not having anywhere to go. Some of the writing was good in a naive, small-town way, and some of it was terrible in a naive, small-town way.

I didn't hear from Joe again for a year. Three days after he came up to the office and told me about everything I had to fly to New York and two weeks later I had to go to London, and from London I had to go to Paris where I had to stay five months. I told Griffis to give Joe as much money as he needed, keep an eye on him, and to let me know how he was making out. Griffis wrote that he hadn't seen Joe again or heard from him. I got back to San Francisco seven months after Joe had come up to the office. Griffis had no idea what had become of Joe.

So I sat down and read his story again. It was no better

and no worse than it had been the first time I had read it. I hoped nothing had happened to him.

A couple more months went by and then one day an airmail letter from Kingsburg came from Joe. He was back home again. He wrote that he had stayed in Frisco only two weeks after borrowing the fifty dollars. Then he'd gone down to Los Angeles where he'd gotten a job on *The Record*. It had lasted three days. Then he'd gone down to El Paso and after that to New Orleans, doing any kind of work he could get and trying to write. After New Orleans he'd gone up to Chicago and gotten a job in a department store, selling sports goods, and three weeks later he'd gone to New York, the one city in the world he'd always wanted to reach. He had been in New York all during the month of August. That was amusing because I had been in New York all during the month of August, too. In New York he'd gotten very homesick for Kingsburg and very tired of big cities and the noise, and one day he'd bought a bus ticket and started back to the old home town. He belonged in Kingsburg, he wrote. He was born there and everybody he knew and liked was born there and he was going to stay there.

Well, as I say, when you go away from home the first time in your life you're usually a year or two under twenty, ambitious and anxious to be a newspaperman or something, eager to meet exciting people and do wonderful things. Everything happens to you. After a while you decide to go home.

That's the first time.

The second time it's different.

That first time away from home you grow older in a couple of months than you do in eighteen years at home. You go home with a heart more or less broken, but after a while everything gets straightened out inside of you and you know enough to make the second departure.

Griffis has been keeping track of Joe for me, and although Joe is still in Kingsburg I know he'll be making his second departure pretty soon.

I'm going to be watching out for him because after that first attempt to live the fine literary life, a guy like Joe is a cinch to do some mighty exciting things. After that first defeat he's not going to be hiding under anybody's *desk*, he's going to be hiding somewhere where he can stand up straight.

Romance

WOULD YOU RATHER sit on this side or would you rather sit on the other side? the red-cap said.

Hmm? the young man said.

This side all right? the red-cap said.

Oh, the young man said. Sure.

He gave the red-cap a dime. The red-cap accepted the small thin coin and folded the young man's coat and placed it on the seat.

Some people like one side, he said, and some like the other.

What? the young man said.

The red-cap didn't know if he ought to go into detail, about some people being used to and preferring certain things in the landscape looking out of the train from one side, and others wanting to get both sides of the landscape all the way down and back, preferring one side going down, usually the shady side, but in some cases the opposite, where a lady liked sunlight or had read it was healthy, and the other side coming up, but he imagined it would take too long to explain everything, especially in view of the fact that he wasn't feeling real well and all morning hadn't been able to give that impression of being on excellent terms with everybody which pleased him so much.

I mean, he said, it's no more than what anybody wants, I guess.

The red-cap figured the young man was a clerk who was going to have a little Sunday holiday, riding in a train from a big city to a little one, going and coming the same day, but what he didn't understand was why the young man seemed so lost, or, as the saying is, dead to the world. The boy was young, not perhaps a college graduate, more likely a boy who'd gone through high school and gotten a job in an office somewhere, maybe twenty-three years old, and perhaps in love. Anyhow, the red-cap thought, the young man looked to be somebody who might at any moment fall in love, without much urging. He had that sad or dreamy look of the potential adorer of something in soft and colorful cloth with long hair and smooth skin.

The young man came to an almost violent awakening which very nearly upset the red-cap.

Oh, he said, I've been sort of day-dreaming.

He wiggled the fingers of his right hand near his head, or where people imagined one day-dreamed.

Have I given you a tip? he said.

The red-cap felt embarrassed.

Yes, sir, he said.

The young man wiggled the fingers of his left hand before his face.

I very often forget what I'm doing, he said, until long

afterwards—sometimes years. May I ask how much I gave you?

The red-cap couldn't figure it out at all. If the young man was being funny or trying to work some sort of a racket, it was just too bad because the red-cap wasn't born yesterday. The young man had given him a dime and if the young man came out with the argument that he had given the red-cap some such ridiculous coin as a five-dollar gold piece the red-cap would simply hold his ground and say, This is all you gave me—this dime.

You gave me a dime, he said.

I'm sorry, the young man said. Here.

He gave the red-cap another dime.

Thank you, sir, the red-cap said.

Were you saying something while we were coming down the aisle? the young man said.

Nothing important, the red-cap said. I was only saying how some folks liked to sit on one side and others on the other.

Oh, the young man said. Is this side all right?

Yes it is, the red-cap said. Unless of course you prefer not getting the sunshine.

No, the young man said, I kind of like sunshine.

It's a fine day too, the red-cap said.

The young man looked out the window as if at the day. There was nothing but trains to see, but he looked out the window as if he were looking to see how fine a day it was.

The sun don't get in here where it's covered up, the red-cap said, but no sooner than you get out of here into

the open you'll be running into a lot of sunshine. Most
California folks get tired of it and get over on the other
side. You from New York?

There was nothing about the young man to suggest
that he was from New York or for that matter from anywhere else either, but the red-cap wondered where the
young man was from, so he asked.

No, the young man said, I've never been out of California.

The red-cap was in no hurry, although there was con-
siderable activity everywhere, people piling into the car,
other red-caps rushing about, helping with bags, and hur-
rying away. Nevertheless, he lingered and carried on a
conversation. There was a girl across the aisle who was
listening to the conversation and the red-cap fancied he
and the young man were cutting quite a figure with her,
one way or another. It was charming conversation, in the
best of spirits, and, although between men in different stations of life, full of that fraternal feeling which is char-
acteristic of westerners and Americans.

I've never been out of California myself, the red-cap
said.

You'd think you'd be the sort of man to travel a good
deal, the young man said.

Yes you would at that, the red-cap said. Working on
trains, or leastaways near them, on and off most of my
life since I was eighteen, which was thirty years ago, but
it's true, I haven't set foot outside the boundary lines of
this state.

I've met a lot of travelers though, he added.

I wouldn't mind getting to New York some day, the young man said.

I don't blame a young man like you for wanting to get to New York, the red-cap said. New York sure must be an interesting place down around in there.

Biggest city in the world, the young man said.

It sure is, the red-cap said, and then he made as if to go, dragging himself away as it were, going away with tremendous regret.

Well, he said, have a pleasant journey.

Thanks, the young man said.

The red-cap left the car. The young man looked out the window and then turned just in time to notice that the girl across the aisle was looking at him and was swiftly turning her head away, and he himself, so as not to embarrass her, swiftly continued turning his head so that something almost happened to his neck. Almost instantly he brought his head all the way back to where it had been, near the window, looking out, and felt an awful eagerness to look at the girl again and at the same time a wonderful sense of at last beginning to go places, in more ways than one, such as meeting people like her and marrying one of them and settling down somewhere in a house somewhere with, more likely than not after time enough, two or three offspring.

He didn't look at the girl again, though, for some time, but kept wanting to very eagerly, so that finally when he did look at her he was embarrassed and blushed and gulped and tried very hard to smile but just couldn't quite make it. The girl just couldn't quite make it either.

That happened after they'd been moving along for more than ten minutes, the train rolling out among the hills and rattling pleasantly and making everything everywhere seem pleasant and full of wonderful potentialities, such as romance and a good deal of good humor and easygoing naturalness, especially insofar as meeting her and being friendly and pleasant and little by little getting to know her and falling in love.

They saw one another again after about seven minutes more, and then again after four minutes, and then they saw one another more steadily by pretending to be looking at the landscape on the other side, and finally they just kept seeing one another steadily for a long time, watching the landscape.

At last the young man said, Are you from New York?

He didn't know what he was saying. He felt foolish and unlike young men in movies who do such things on trains.

Yes, I am, the girl said.

What? the young man said.

Didn't you ask if I was from New York? the girl said.

Oh, the young man said. Yes, I did.

Well, the girl said, I am.

I didn't know you were from New York, the young man said.

I know you didn't, the girl said.

The young man tried very hard to smile the way they smiled in pictures.

How did you know? he said.

Oh I don't know, the girl said. Are you going to Sacramento?

Yes, I am, the young man said. Are you?

Yes, I am, the girl said.

What are you doing so far from home? the young man said.

New York isn't my home, the girl said. I was born there but I've been living in San Francisco most of my life.

So have I most of mine, the young man said. In fact all of it.

I've lived in San Francisco practically all of my life too, the girl said, with the possible exception of them few months in New York.

Is that all the time you lived in New York? the young man said.

Yes, the girl said, only them first five months right after I was born in New York.

I was born in San Francisco, the young man said. There's lots of room on these two seats, he said with great effort. Wouldn't you like to sit over here and get the sun?

All right, the girl said.

She stepped across the aisle and sat across from the young man.

I just thought I'd go down to Sacramento on the special Sunday rate, the young man said.

I've been to Sacramento three times, the girl said.

The young man began to feel very happy. The sun was strong and warm and the girl was wonderful. Unless he was badly mistaken, or unless he got fired Monday morning, or unless America got into a war and he had to become a soldier and go away and get himself killed for no good reason, he had a hunch some day he would go to work and get acquainted with the girl and marry her and settle down.

He sat back in the sunlight while the train rattled along and smiled romantically at the girl, getting ready for the romance.

At the Chop Suey Joint on Larkin Street at Two Thirty in the Morning

THIS WAS A place that didn't do a nickel's worth of business till after ten o'clock at night; mostly low-lifes of the region; five not-very-Chinese-looking Chinese, that is, not truly Chinese any longer, kind of spoiled after too many years in that neighborhood, a little too close to American tragedy and scum and vulgarity; that is, they'd lost the East in themselves, they'd become Western, kind of snappy in a way, kind of efficient, talkative, which is not the true Chinese way. In the Chinese restaurants in Chinatown of Frisco, where the Chinese are truly Chinese, the waiters aren't that way, they're quiet, self-respecting, unhurried, partly deaf, and yet at the same time, not at all offensive, they don't make you dislike them, like the boys in this joint do, who, to all appearances, are the friendliest souls in the world. It just doesn't seem to work, some reason or other.

Anyhow, Terranova and I had just walked a friend home, after a night of dull conversationally brilliant people who had griped Terranova, and much drinking, and now he was hungry, so when he saw the Chop Suey sign he thought he'd like some tomato beef which when cooked right is something good to eat.

It was half past two in the morning and when we got to the door we saw the good-looking young man and the smart Chinese waiter making a commotion. You could just tell trouble was going on, so Terranova, who was feeling disgusted on account of the lousy conversation all evening, went in and we took the table next to the young man's.

Look at the poor guy, Terranova said. He's so lonely he's got to make trouble about the price of something he ate in a joint like this.

The Chinese waiter was growing severe, in a sort of American bouncer way, and he said, You pay thirty-five cents or I call police.

The young man got more indignant and said, Go ahead, call the police.

He wants to see them, Terranova said. He wants *them* to see *him*. It's all on account of loneliness. Who wants to argue about thirty-five cents? Ten to one he's got more money than you and me put together.

How do you know? I said.

You're dumber than the people you introduced me to tonight, Terranova said. He's lonely, can't you see? It's not the money. He wants them to make a fuss over him. Look how pretty he is.

I looked, and sure enough he was pretty. He was soft all over and indignant like a woman with trouble going on in her.

The Chinese waiter came close to grabbing the young man by the neck and the young man kind of challenged him to do it, but he didn't after all.

You pay, he said, or I call police.

I won't pay, the young man said.

So the Chinese waiter stepped out to the sidewalk and in less than two minutes two big cops came in, kind of business-like. They had been in the beer joint next door. They were like the Chinese too, kind of spoiled by the neighborhood, easy work, and lots of money from the joints.

They were big, though, and that was what counted.

All right, the biggest one said to the young man, you ate, so pay or I'll run you in.

Well, said the young man, you can see for yourself from these dishes on the table that I didn't have thirty-five cents' worth.

The big cop looked over at his friend and smiled and the other one smiled back, then made one of them faces that means, Well, shut my mouth, look what we've got here.

Oh, the big cop said. Oh, I see. You didn't have thirty-five cents' worth. Well, what is thirty-five cents' worth? Come on, give this young Chinese boy his thirty-five cents and take a walk.

Well, it isn't fair, the young man said.

Come on, *pay*, the cop said. Come on. Come on, he said like a comedian.

He didn't touch the young man and for a moment the young man waited.

Then he got up and brought some currency from his pocket.

Terranova hit my arm and said, See? I win.

He gave the Chinese waiter a five dollar bill, and the cop said, That's a good boy.

The two of them went back to the kitchen to eat something free.

The Chinese waiter came back in a moment with the change. All of it was silver, the way it is in Frisco always. The young man put the money in his pocket, but dropped a half dollar.

The Chinese waiter picked it up and offered it to him.

Keep it, the young man said.

It wasn't easy to figure out why. The Chinese waiter couldn't figure it out either, and the young man went away. The waiter giggled and went back to the kitchen and then the cops roared with laughter.

Ohio

IT'S A SAD world, Sam said. He was playing *I've Got a Feeling You're Fooling*, smoking a nickel cigar, keeping his eyes on the gobs and talking to a kid who'd come into the place for the first time with a slick dame and was now drunk and sorry about everything.

Sad? said the kid. It's worse than sad, it's lousy. It's ten times lousier than Ohio.

Ohio? said Sam, tickling the piano keys, punctuating his question with a lot of loud chords. Ohio? What the hell's Ohio got to do with the world?

The gobs were waltzing all over the place, bending the girls this way and the other, hugging them like maybe they would finish the job right there while they were dancing.

Ohio? said the kid. What's Ohio got to do with the world? Ohio *is* the world, pal. I was *born* in Ohio.

Well, said Sam. I'm mighty glad to speak to a man who was born in Ohio. Myself I was born incognito, ha-ha-ha.

That's funny, said the kid. Ha-ha-ha, he said. That's *very* funny.

What's the matter? Sam said.

What's the matter? said the kid. Everything's the matter.

Is it that dame? said Sam. Well, take it easy. She ain't much.

Not much she ain't much, said the kid. She's Ohio and everywhere else to me.

She's a pushover, son, said Sam. Take it easy.

He knew the kid was worried because the girl was waltzing around with one of the gobs.

Pushover? said the kid. Don't give me any of that kind of lip. Don't talk about *my* girl in that kind of language.

Your girl? said Sam, breaking into *Miss Otis Regrets*.

You're goofy, boy. That girl is your girl and my girl and the gob's girl. She belongs to any man in the world who can buy her a drink.

The kid told Sam to go to hell and went over to the bar. Sam saw him swallow a drink the way young kids who are being disillusioned do it.

Poor kid, he said.

He saw the kid's dame swimming around over the floor with the big gob.

He played one more number, *Cheek to Cheek,* and then had Mike bring him a bottle of beer. He didn't want the beer, he wanted the bottle. He poured the beer into a glass and put the glass on the piano. He put the bottle under the piano where it would be handy.

Them young fools always made trouble because they took things too seriously.

If Sam, the piano player, had to break somebody's head, he had to, that was all, and he'd do it, even if it hurt him more than it hurt (a) the kid, or (b) the gob, or (c) the girl.

He didn't like to hit anybody over the head with a beer bottle, but he never took time out to dwell on the moral aspects of the act when the trouble started. There was something fine about grabbing the bottle firmly by the neck, swinging it upward, bringing it down on a befuddled head, bringing order and poise into the universe again, going back to the piano while Mike dragged the fellow to the street, and playing, as if nothing was changed anywhere in the world and all was well, *The Music Goes Round and Round*.

He began to play the song, looking around, watching the boy, knowing the trouble would start soon, and he would bend down, lift the bottle, walk to where the trouble was, and stop it.

The War in Spain

YOU COULD BARELY breathe it was so sultry.

My big brother Drake was in his room, walking around naked after a cold bath, talking out loud and singing. Take everything, he said.

Take my money.

My heart.

Take my life, he said.

I slumped down in the rocking-chair on the front porch and watched him. This is a sad year in the world, I thought. I could feel the world laughing at all of us who are alive.

Drake stood in his room, smoking a cigarette.

You know you belong to somebody else, he sang. So *why* don't you leave me alone?

Then he busted out laughing.

Enoch, he called. Oh, Enoch.

I got up from the rocking-chair and went into the house. Pa was sleeping on the couch in the parlor. He looked as if he were trying to get far away to a place where he could breathe clear air.

I went into Drake's room.

What? I said.

Enoch, he said.

What?

What are you dreaming about *now?*

Nothing, I said. What do you want?

My boy, he said. I'll be leaving you soon. I want to have a little talk with you.

This is the saddest year of the world, I thought.

Where you going? I said.

Enoch, my boy, he said. I'm on my way to the war.

War? I said. You're fooling.

I was scared, like the times when I'd think the world would end in a minute or two, everything break to pieces and everybody die, drowning or suffocating or being crushed by some great unseen weight.

You're fooling, I said.

My boy, he said, I am now a soldier.

I started to cry because I could tell he wasn't fooling. He lifted me off the floor and dropped me face down on his bed.

Enoch, my boy, he said, war is man's delight. Danger is his solace, and death is the lover of all who breathe.

He talked a long time. I sat up and looked at him. In a war, I thought, a man is killed. Drake will be killed.

They'll kill you in the war, I said. Don't go, Drake.

Maybe they'll kill me, and maybe they won't, he said. That's what I want to find out.

They'll kill you, I said.

I saw him dead in the middle of some dark earthly

desolation and began to cry. He would be alone there and broken, his body crushed. Ma heard me crying and came to the room.

Why are you making the boy cry? she said.

They'll kill him, I bawled. Drake's going to the war in Spain, and they'll kill him.

Ma screamed. Drake, she cried.

Drake puffed at his cigarette.

Drake, Drake, Drake, Ma cried.

She turned and ran to Pa.

Enoch, my boy, said Drake, I want to leave you anything of mine you'd care to have. My gun, my phonograph, my books. I'll talk to Paula later. You come first.

I don't want anything, I bawled. They'll kill you. You wait and see.

You're nine, he said. That's a good age for music. I'll leave you the phonograph and the records. How will that be?

No, I said. I don't want anything.

Paula can have the books, he said. Go call her.

I was glad to go. I ran up the stairs to Paula's room.

Drake is going to the war, I said.

I didn't wait for Paula to say anything. I ran out of the room, and she came down the stairs a moment later. Pa and Ma were in Drake's room, talking to him. Paula was Drake's twin and she didn't seem sorry at all. I guess she understood Drake too well to believe what he was doing was wrong.

I followed her into the room. Ma was still crying, but Pa only looked tired.

You're not old enough to go to the war, he said.

I took care of that, Drake said.

He looked at Paula.

You can have my books, he said.

You're only eighteen, Ma said, and she started to cry again.

Only? Drake said.

You're no Communist, Pa said.

I'm a student, Drake said.

Don't cry, Ma, Paula said. Nothing'll happen to Drake.

Sure, said Drake.

He'll be killed, I said.

What do you want to be a soldier for? Pa said.

Drake put on his coat and hat, smiling at everybody, and Ma started to cry louder than ever.

Pa said, God damn it.

He put his arms around Ma and said, What do you want to cry for?

He took Ma into the parlor.

That was all. Drake went to the war. We never saw him again, and nobody in the house except Paula could keep from crying. Paula kept saying, *They can't kill Drake,* even though he was dead.

Comedy is Where You Die and They Don't Bury You Because You Can Still Walk

ALL NIGHT INSTEAD of sleeping he stared out of the lower berth window at the dark sky and remembered for the first time in many years his oldest dreams. He looked far away into heaven, looking far away into his heart, and felt the regret within himself at the hours and days and years wasted, the warm days of summer lost, the heavy ripe air unbreathed, the years empty of everything but roaring streets and crazy people, the eye blind to everything but ugliness, the ear deaf to everything but noise, the heart dead to everything but struggle.

For hours he watched the dark land, hungering for it. The level plains, the bare hills, the lonely brooding trees.

My God, he said.

He began to dream, his heart talking to itself.

Seven times the sheep have wakened and seven times it is the same afternoon. There is still light upon the earth.

A ferocious hunger for food possessed him. He got into his clothes and went looking for the porter. He found the Negro sleeping in the smoking room. He sat down and lighted a cigarette. After five minutes, when the porter did not waken, he shook the man and said, I'm sorry, but I'm hungry. Can you get me some food?

There ain't no food at this hour, the porter said.

He brought some money from his pocket and handed the porter two one-dollar bills.

Get me a lot of sandwiches, he said, and anything to drink you can find.

Any kind of sandwiches? the porter said.

Yes, he said.

You want to spend all this money? the porter said.

I want food, he said. Anything you can get.

There ain't no place to eat at this hour, the porter said.

I'll eat here, he said. Get anything you can. Here's a dollar for yourself.

I'll do the best I can, the porter said.

The porter stayed away almost half an hour. He returned at last with seven sandwiches and six bottles of various kinds of soda pop.

This is the best I could do, he said.

Thanks, the young man said. Did you bring a bottle-opener?

Yes, sir, the porter said. I didn't forget no bottle-opener at this hour of the night.

The porter put down the sandwiches and the bottles and went away.

The young man unwrapped one of the sandwiches, opened one of the bottles, and began to eat and drink.

He began to feel better, less conscious of the wasted years, less grieved by death within himself. Eating and drinking, he began to feel amused. The world was all right. It was hard, but it had to be hard. It killed you, but it did so innocently, without motive. He knew he was dead, but nobody could prove it. Nobody knew.

Suddenly, while he was eating, he heard his heart again and the food became poison. It became like ash and he could not swallow. He got up as if someone had entered the room and saw only himself in the mirror. He spat the food from his mouth and listened.

Seven times, his heart said.

What the hell is this anyway? he said.

He sat down and lighted a cigarette. His heart talked on, and he sat like a small child, listening, and while his heart talked, he argued with it.

Let them waken seven *hundred* times, he said. Nothing can kill me. In the morning this train will reach San Francisco.

He tried to eat again, but the miserable food wouldn't go down.

I remember, his heart said.

His guts choked with nausea, and bending with the pain, he waited for the murder to end, so he could breathe again.

He straightened at last, dried his eyes, and began to laugh in memory at the wretched comedy of mortal man in the immortal world. The world alive and inhuman, the man human and dead. The slapstick comedy of his hunger to live, to open the eye to something better than ugliness, to silence the roaring streets, to fill the empty years with light and reality.

He was still laughing when he reached his berth, stretched out, and looked far away into heaven again. Now dead, his heart said, *Go ahead and laugh. What else can you do?*

Noonday Dark Enfolding Texas

WHEN WINTER ENDED in 1935 a lot of earth was lifted by wind and carried from one place to another, making a dust storm. If there hadn't been cities on this continent, this natural event wouldn't have made much difference one way or another, but there *were* cities.

The first thing they teach us at school is that earth is not for breathing. We are not rodents or reptiles or worms. We do not burrow into the earth. Our life is not sustained by darkness, it is sustained by light. It is not hidden in density, it is reflected in transparency. Our substance is refreshed and renewed by air and water and light.

The second thing they teach us is that there was a flood once on the earth. It was a mythical flood or a small flood much exaggerated by men who feared God. It doesn't matter. The living perished in that flood; the living, at least, which were not fish. The flood was supposed to be punishment. There was much ungodliness among the living, so the living were drowned. This is perhaps no more than a fable. Even so it is a good one. Evil is as well destroyed by flood as by fire or anything else natural. But where's the evil in being alive in a small town in America?

Dry, desolate and lonely Texas, rock and sand and dust, and the train. Lord God the crazy train rattling through Texas, the sky dark with dust and the smoker full of the sad faces, the travelers, the everlasting travelers of the earth, going from one place to another, leaving one thing for another, and seeking God only knows what.

If you like, of course you can dismiss the whole thing by saying trains are saddening. One shouldn't get aboard a train. One should walk. One shouldn't go from one place to another. One should stay in one place, and let it go at that.

I'll agree that trains are tragic contraptions. I'll agree that going from one place to another is a melancholy activity.

Even so.

I myself, aboard the train, had no destination. The train, however, was going to El Paso. So, with the train, my destination was, in a way, El Paso.

El Paso.

Lord God. I'd never seen the city. I knew El Paso was a city because it came up in geography one year. It didn't come up in mythology. It wasn't a buried city or a mythical city, it was a place in Texas. The living had made this place only recently, especially the Americans. I don't know for sure, but maybe a dozen cities have been buried under the place where El Paso now stands, cities of Mexicans and Indians. I'm only guessing, not being a student. But El Paso itself was one of the *American* cities that came up in geography. We used to learn something significant about every city and state in America. Pittsburgh, coal. Nebraska, wheat. Kansas, corn. Boston, culture. And so on. I never did remember what we learned about El Paso. I knew Texas was big. I knew it was cattle country and all that, but I didn't know anything specific about El Paso. I figured it was a place in the world, inhabited by the living and therefore a place of the holy presence of God on earth.

What I mean is, living, are we to live, or not? Geographically and mythically, religiously, and every other way. Are we to live, living, or are we to be fretted to death by trains and dust storms, blizzards and floods and fires, hunger and pain, labor and fear, debts and entanglements, cold and homelessness, monotony and noise? Is our presence here to be something, or nothing? In this experience of hydrogen and oxygen, earth and water and fire, time and space, are we to reach any place, are we to know any truth, are we to possess any loveliness? Or what? Lord God, I'm in earnest. I wanted to know that year, and I want to know this year.

Is it full of meaning because the meaning is nothing and we will be pleased to have nothing, bread and shelter and clothing and water and warmth, a place to walk, and a place to pause and rest? And is it meaningless because the meaning we want is more than we can have? It's fine: it's the world. You're born and you become the center of a multitude of encumbrances. You work, you die. Brother, there's meaning for you, but you know it's no meaning to write home about. You know it's the easiest and goofiest meaning to be had. The most scientific, the most real. That's all: the world. Take it or leave it. And you take it. You break even.

What are we going to get out of it? What *can* we get out of it? Well, we can get one of two things: nothing, or everything. If you're religious, you know this is so. Unseeking you can have nothing and at the same time much that isn't worth tabulating, or, seeking, you can seek love, and maybe find it, as I did in El Paso.

I had no place to go that year, but I was on the train and so were a lot of other people. The train roared through the dust of the southwest, and the dust came into the train. Your nostrils became dry, your lungs became dry, your hands became dry, and you asked the question. You looked at the earth, desolate Texas, and asked the question. Even here, Lord? Even *out* of this dryness, in the midst of this desolation? That loveliness, Thy presence? There have been births in Texas, Lord.

I remember the men in the smoking car talking, but I don't remember what they said. It was about trouble. I remember buying a Texas paper and reading a headline: *Noonday Dark Enfolding Texas.* I remember a photograph of a man who had died, a Texas Judge. I remember he was a remarkable Judge in that he overruled or sustained objections as a baseball referee declares a player safe or out, using the baseball gestures, both arms outspread for objection sustained, thumb high for objection overruled. A great American, direct, no hocus-pocus: you're out, you're safe. Now, he himself was out, and the old thumb was high.

The train came into El Paso, and I got off.

It was dark in El Paso that day at two in the afternoon. It was the storm, the dust. You couldn't breathe,
and there was a strong wind. Even so, there it was, El
Paso, which I had never before seen. It was the ugliest and
loveliest city I have ever seen. If you looked at the buildings and streets, it was ugly, as all cities are, but if you
looked beyond the buildings and streets at God there, the
living, it was lovely. It was night and day in Texas the
day I reached there. No sun, no light, no transparency. We
don't stay here long. We aren't allowed to stay long. It was
a dead city, it was part of a dead world, a dead age, a
universe dying, aching with loneliness, gasping for breath.
That is a thing that frightens you. That makes you want
life the worst way. I jumped into a cab. The next train
wouldn't be leaving El Paso for five or six hours, and in a
dust storm, on this continent, in Texas, five or six hours
is a long long time.

Take me to the best hotel in town, I said.

I went up to a room and took off the dusty clothes
and washed the dust out of my skin. There was a lot of fine
dust in the room, even though the windows were shut.
The dust got in just the same. It was one of those immediate things you couldn't do anything about, except ignore,
and you *can't* ignore immediate things until you're dead,
which is a thing you don't like to be while you're alive. I
went down to the street and began walking through the
beautiful, ugly, dying city. The girls were like the girls of
all places, only different. They were Texas, but different
from ever before. They were Texas in the sudden darkness
of noonday; enfolded in the dark; sealed in the far away

dream. One of them was the one I was seeking, and knew she was, so that, even in that desolation, there was meaning at last to write home about. Afterwards, on the train, going away from Texas, rolling out of the dream, I listened to the men in the smoker roaring with the lonely laughter of the living, and suddenly I began to cry, roaring with laughter, because I knew we were all dead, didn't know it, and therefore couldn't do anything about it.

Johnny the Dreamer, Mary the Model at Magnin's, and Plato the Democrat

THE BAR WAS crowded, the tables were all taken, and the place was full of smoke and noise. The best I could do was share a small table with a young man who'd been drinking for some time. Although he was alone, he was talking when I sat down. I had a half hour to kill, so I sat down and listened to him.

I drowned my sorrows with a girl named Mary once who used to be a model at Magnin's, he said. Ten years ago. I used to have to drown my sorrows every season in those days. When I say seasons I don't mean just the seasons of the year, I mean the fishing season, the football season, the opera season, and all the other seasons. I remember the terrible sorrow I had to drown once during the society season. It wasn't the easiest thing to do because of the pronunciation, which was embarrassing for me to listen to and more embarrassing for me to try to approximate, as it were. Ghastly is a simple word for me during the fishing season, but during the society season it's *ghastly*. Of course I can pronounce ghastly in the society manner

as well as the next man. Interesting is another word I can
pronounce the society way. I learned quite a few of them.
Ghastly, interesting, divine, chambertin, ecstatic, *élan*,
André Gide, *bon mot*, and dozens of others.

The society season began for me that year in September, in the lobby of the De Luxe Hotel on Grant Avenue
near Broadway, where I had a suite of one room and bath
down the hall, and ended four days later in the Sky Room
or the Starlight Room or some name like that of The
Empire Hotel. There I finally sent the sorrows down for
the third time, drowned them, and was carried out of the
building by three friends, college men and each of them
all-around good fellows.

Mary was in the swim of things with me during that
time of sorrow and always held up my spirits when it
seemed like the weight of my grief was too much for me
to carry alone. My tragedy during the sorrow of the
society season was the consequence of a stretch of bad
luck at gambling, with disappearance of much-needed
money. Money I needed, I must say, for the barest necessi-
ties of life. Bread and water and a pinch of salt. At last
the tragedy was just too much. It suddenly became a
matter of either the tragedy or myself. One of us had to
go. The war was waged fair and square and I won. That is,
Mary won. She did all the quarreling with the tragedy,
squared off beautifully, jockeyed into contention, and fired
away like mad—after which the tragedy got dressed,
packed a bag and went in search of a cousin of mine named
Nick who had a smile that could melt a heart of stone.

Mary was always glad to do it. Johnny, she always used

to say, I've got all the faith in the world in you and any time things look gloomy, you just come to me and we'll sit down and straighten everything out. She used to say dozens and dozens of other nice things, too.

We were the most platonic friends in the world. You hear a lot of talk about platonic friendships, but probably no more than one platonic friendship out of a hundred is the real thing. With a bottle on the floor, a fire roaring in the fireplace and the phonograph playing Debussy, Mary used to read Plato to me for hours. I can remember lying back in the deepest sorrow and just listening to Mary reading, *Next then, I suppose, we must examine Democracy and find out how it arises and what it is like, so that we may know what the democratic man is like and estimate his value.*

I used to lie back and dream about what the democratic man is like, and then I'd just move back an inch or two more, and estimate his value. He would be like a fellow I knew once named Luke who always said all he knew was that he was a Democrat and wanted no trouble with nobody, just so they'd leave him alone. I estimated his value at ten cents a pound. He was a small man, and all told came to about $14.35 with his clothes on.

Plato was a real sweetheart to both of us in those days. Mary was improving her mind all the time because of the type of people she was meeting at Magnin's, who imagined themselves superior to Mary, not only in breeding but in education.

As a matter of fact, if the truth were known, Mary was always the best-bred of the lot, and for my money the best-educated. She was built like a Debussy daydream in a 1924 custom-built Stutz. But the debutantes and their mothers who came to Magnin's for their clothes hurt Mary's feelings, so she went and bought the collected works of Plato.

Every once in a while after I got through dreaming about what the democratic man is like, I would wonder what *Plato* himself was like and what his first name was.

What's his first name, Mary? I used to say.

First name? Mary used to say. Why, I don't know. They just called him Plato.

What was he, anyhow?

He was a philosopher. All this stuff I'm reading is philosophy.

Is that what it is?

Of course.

Well, I guess lots of stuff is philosophy and nobody stops to notice.

This is all *Plato's* philosophy.

It sure is nice to know, I used to say. Read some more.

So Mary used to go back to the book and read.

But the money-makers fix their eyes on the ground and pretend not to see; instead they go on poisoning with their wealth any of the other citizens who give up the struggle, and increase the number of drones and beggars in the city. While, as for themselves and their own sons, their young men are luxurious and useless both in mind and body, lazy and too soft to endure pain or resist pleasure.

She used to read, *When the ruling class and the ruled*

meet one another in the streets or at public meetings, at festivals or in the army, when they serve side by side either on board ship or in the ranks and see one another facing danger, the poor will not be despised by the rich. On the contrary, often a poor man, strong and brown, stands in the ranks next to a rich man, who has lived an indoor life and is far too fat; and, seeing his shortness of breath and general discomfort, will surely think that such men as these are rich simply because the poorer classes are cowards. And whenever he meets his friends the word will get passed around. We can do what we like with these men; they are good for nothing.

And my God I used to lie back on the floor at Mary's and just listen and listen to all that wonderful stuff that was philosophy.

I am quite sure, Mary would go on reading, *that they will.*

Now wait a minute, Mary, I used to say. Just let me get that straight. Will *what?*

Why, they will do what they like with the rich men, Mary would say.

Well, I used to say, what do you suppose they want to do with them?

Well, I'll read and find out, Mary used to say.

Well then, I suppose, she'd go on reading, *democracy comes into existence when the poor have conquered the rich, killing some, banishing others, and sharing citizenship and office with the rest.*

I see, I used to say. Good. Read some more.

So Mary used to go on.

That is how democracy is established, whether it be through armed force or whether the opposite side give in at once through fear.

That would make me jump to my feet and say, Well, by God, how long has this been going on?

This is all ancient stuff, Mary used to say. This was written before Christ.

No fooling?

Of course.

Well, that's different, I used to say. Just so they don't come around and try to scare *me* with their armed force.

Scare *you?* Mary used to say. Why, Johnny, you're not rich.

That doesn't make any difference. Suppose I get rich some day?

Well, all right, Mary used to say. Just rest, and let me go on reading.

O. K.

Well, now, Mary used to go on reading, *how will they live and what kind of a government will theirs be? First, of course, they are free, and the city is full of freedom and free speech and every one may do whatever he wishes.*

And where everyone may do as he wishes it is quite clear that each man will order his own life in the way that pleases him best.

So, I imagine, under this government we shall find men of all sorts and kinds.

Certainly.

Then this is likely to be a very beautiful form of government.

Along about this time I'd swim off to sleep and wake up just in time to come in on, *Is not this a gloriously pleasant kind of life for the moment?*

Perhaps for the moment.

And how considerate such a city is. No nonsense there about trifles.

It is wonderful.

It seems to be a pleasant form of government, varied and without rulers, dealing out its own special brand of equality to equal and unequal alike.

Mary used to read Plato to me all the time in those days of sorrow. She wanted to improve her mind so she could talk down to the society riff-raff that was always trying to make her feel cheap.

Finally one day in the Geranium Room or something like that at the Harry Hopkins Hotel or some place like that, at the bar, Mary put a young loafer in his place who thought he could get away with etching-talk with a girl like her, brought up platonically. He was one of them boys who even before Christ were too lazy and too soft to endure pain or resist pleasure, and he passed a few intimate remarks to Mary who listened carefully, reflected on what the democratic man is like, weighed his value, considered the sum involved, and then said, You can talk that way to your society friends, my good fellow, but you can't talk that way to *me*—a model at Magnin's.

She was a sweetheart of a girl.

The drinker stopped a moment to remember what a sweetheart of a girl Mary was. Then he said, I remember the sorrow I drowned with her during the Horse Show season. . . .

Wait a minute, I said. It was time for me to go and I wanted to know more about Mary herself. Let's not rush into the sorrow you drowned with her during the Horse Show season. Tell me about Mary herself. What was her last name?

What? he said.

Her last name? I said.

Who's last name?

Mary's.

Mary who?

Your friend, the model at Magnin's, I said. The girl you used to drown your sorrow with.

What are you talking about, he said?

You were telling me about a girl named Mary that you used to drown your sorrow with, I said.

I've been quoting Plato, he said.

O. K., I said. It doesn't matter. It's been nice drinking with you.

You call yourself a drinker? he said. I used to pal around with a guy named Felix like you once in Boston. He was an Austrian on his father's side and an American on his mother's side. Claimed he was a child prodigy. Said he'd studied ten years. He was twenty-one but looked younger because he shaved every day. He always carried a violin around with him. Not in a case. Out in the open. The violin in one hand and the bow in the other. He used to wear short pants. I never could figure out why he wanted to be a child prodigy. I met his son, too. He was a nice-looking little boy, five years old, and he had his own little violin, right out in the open, too, and his own bow. When I saw the boy I told the father to sit down and put the lousy violin away for a minute and have a drink, but he wouldn't do it. He claimed he had to keep up with his studies if he ever intended to get anywhere in the world.

I'm sorry, I said. I've got to go now. I'd like to hear the whole story about Felix, but I'm late.

What's the matter? he said.

I've been sick, I said. I can't have more than seven without feeling a little confused. So long.

So long, he said.

He went right on talking—to God, most likely, who is a better listener than I am.

The Best and Worst People and Things of 1938

THE FIRST THING to do, Joe said, is to decide who was the worst person of the year.

Well, Pete said, we may not know. There may have been somebody somewhere who was the worst and nobody heard about it.

Joe closed his eyes and retreated into memory.

The worst *we* know about, he said with his eyes shut. From the newspapers, the radio, or any other medium of communication.

He opened his eyes with a mechanical swiftness, as if they were part of a camera, and as if he needed to be very swift if he expected to find out if his friend had caught on to the idea.

It was obvious that his friend had.

What do we want to do that for? Pete said, nevertheless.

Joe became very amazed. He wiggled an irritated and terribly impatient right hand at his friend, while Pete smiled and shook his head in wonder at the goofy and useless seriousness of the other.

No reason in the world, Joe said. It's December. It's 1938. This is the season for selecting the worst and best of everything. *The Nation* will come out with its list in the next issue or two. Lots of other people will review the year and try to understand what happened. It's raining. The year's almost over. It was a good year. We're in this hightone bar, drinking Scotch. You know and I know what's going on everywhere. The least we can do is say something about it, and choose up teams. Who would you say was Heel Number One of the year?

Pete was only amused.

Not counting you? he said.

When was I a heel in 1938? Joe said.

What about Esther Ramirez? Pete said.

That was late in 1937, Joe said, and she was no more your girl than she was mine. I did you a favor. I nominate Hitler.

Too easy, Pete said. Anybody can nominate Hitler. Chamberlain would be better.

That Munich affair *had* to be the way it was, Joe said. Chamberlain was no fool.

He was a rat, Pete said.

I stick to Hitler, Joe said.

Well, even if you do, Pete said, it's no good. Hitler's been that way for years. It's nothing new this year.

Pete swallowed the rest of his drink and added, What you're talking about is Fascism anyway; not Hitler. This kind of talk is chit-chat. We all know we don't like Fascism. Saying we don't doesn't mean anything. Want to know something?

Joe nodded several times, disgusted.

Fascism is disgusted with itself, Pete said. It hates itself.

Boy, Joe said, you're some philosopher. You sure understand everything, don't you?

I can carry on a barroom conversation as well as anybody, Pete said.

The waiter brought fresh drinks. It was the fifth for each of them.

You know what I mean, though, Joe said. What about all this stuff?

I say the hell with it, Pete said.

Is that all you say?

Sure, Pete said. That's all.

It's going to be a fine world with that kind of talk going on, Joe said.

Fine or lousy, Pete said, I say the hell with it. I don't intend to do anything about it. All I've ever done has been for myself. I'm no hero and I've got no ambition to be one. That's a disease too. Being a hero about what you think is right is what all the heroes are doing, some on one side, and some on the other. No hero doesn't believe he's on the right side. As far as I'm concerned, if there's got to be sides, every side is right, and wrong. And the heroes are all sick.

If you ain't a hero, what are you? Joe said.

I'm a loafer and a Presbyterian, Pete said. What are you?

To tell you the truth, Joe said, that's what I am too, only I belong to The Leap-to-Glory sect of the Baptist denomination; I'm also a jockey.

On a wooden horse, Pete said. You're riding down the fox in a small circle. But so are a couple of million others. It's all right. So who's Heel Number One of the world this year?

Nobody, I guess, Joe said.

I think you're right, Pete said. There is no heel like that. It's all chit-chat. The world is riding down the fox in a small circle too. The thing to do is let it ride. Let it think it's really getting somewhere. It's all Hi-yo, Silver.

Sure, Joe said. Who was the *best* person of the year?

That'll turn out the same way, Pete said. There was no best person of the year. They were all lousy; and all right too. You've got this thing figured out wrong. You're short-sighted. You're also unimaginative. Run them *all* together and you've still got something pathetic.

I didn't know, Joe said. In that case I guess we'd better just drink and start making phone calls.

That's right, Pete said.

O. K., Joe said. Who was best for you in 1938?

I won't tell, Pete said.

Will you tell me who was worst? Joe said.

Of course not, Pete said.

Why not? Joe said.

Well, I'll tell you, Pete said. Because the best and the worst are the same. What are we, idiots, or what? Don't we know anything?

We know how to read, Joe said.

The waiter brought two more and took away the empty glasses.

Pete lifted his glass to Joe. Here's to you, Joe, he said.

Pete, Joe said, lifting his glass. Here's to me.

That's right, Pete said. And here's to me.

That's all anybody can drink to, Joe said.

For the most part, yes, Pete said, and the sooner they find out the better.

Here's to their finding out soon, Joe said.

That's a prayer, not a toast, Pete said.

In that case, Joe said, let's close our eyes, fold our hands and bow our heads.

And start telephoning, Pete said.

Joe prayed for half a minute.

Amen, he said. He opened his eyes, lifted his bowed head, and swallowed some more of his drink.

What were the best and worst things of the year? he said.

All of them, Pete said. All of them. All of them. Don't ask questions like a child.

He got up from the table and fished in his pocket for nickels.

I'm going to begin phoning, he said.

He walked out of the barroom into the hall where the row of four phone booths were and heard the music coming from the Persian or Greek or Ethiopian or Jewish or Czechoslovakian Room. He leaned against one of the booths a moment, listening, then went in, closed the door, and began dialing. At the table his friend was saying to himself that if it was so, it was lousy and he would make no phone calls at all.

None whatsoever.

He'd just sit there and drink until two in the morning, dial nobody, and the hell with everything and everybody.

What We Want is Love and Money

WHAT'S YOUR NAME? she said.

Joe, he said. We met last night at Musso & Frank's.

Oh yes of course, she said. How silly of me to forget. You're a writer.

You can forget that, he said.

My husband told me, she said.

All right, I'm a writer.

You must be pretty good.

Pretty bad, he said, but better than most. Let's forget it.

You don't like writers, do you?

They're all right. Have another drink?

All right.

Two more, he said to the bartender.

O. K., said the bartender.

Do you like it here? she said.

It's swell, he said.

Why do you dislike it? she said.

No, he said, I mean it. It's swell. I've always got money here.

He smiled foolishly, a little amused.

What are you grinning about? she said.

Money, he said, and me.

You've been poor?

Poverty-stricken, he said. Constantly without funds. Ill-clothed.

That's a nice suit you're wearing, she said.

First suit I ever had made to order, he said. I never knew clothes could be so comfortable. Cost me seventy-five bucks.

He smiled to himself.

I didn't earn the money, though, he said.

Who you with? she said.

Paramount, he said. Good old Paramount. Giving me a lot of dough for nothing. They think it's an honor too. I ain't complaining.

Got a good assignment?

Swell.

Really? she said, Or are you kidding again?

I haven't been kidding, he said. See these shoes? Cost me eighteen bucks. Supposed to be the best.

What kind of a story is it? she said.

Well, he said, it's hard to tell. I think it's standard.

Standard? she said. What's that?

You know, he said. What they want is love and money.

Who?

The boy and the girl.

Oh, the girl said. Is it a comedy?

An hilarious one, he said.

Really?

It's fairly side-splitting, he said.

I don't believe you, she said. Do you always talk double-talk?

Double-talk? he said. What's that?

Oh you know, she said. You've been talking double-talk all the time.

I didn't know that, he said.

I guess I'm drunk, he said.

The girl busted out laughing.

You, drunk? she said. You're soberer than anybody in this place. You're soberer, I might say, than anybody in Hollywood.

DRUNK she roared with laughter. You're probably the soberest writer on the North American Continent. You're soberer than anybody in the whole world. You're wonderful.

My God, the young man thought, where the hell's her husband? She's cockeyed. Myself, all *I* want is money.

The Sweet Singer of Omsk

THERE IS A Russian from Omsk in this town, Hollywood, who is a singer. He has read my books and claims I do not know what I have written. He claims *he* knows. He claims he is my best reader and he says I myself, Saroyan, Wheelyam Sar-o-yan, as he says, do not understand my stuff, which I wrote.

He is a serious man, an excellent singer of Russian songs, expert on the guitar, deeply sorrowful, extremely courteous, extraordinarily unhappy. He claims he is dead, not alive. He asks how I, writing as I do, saying what I say, am able to be so much alive. I tell him I don't know.

He then declares that I do not know what I write.

He plays the guitar like a crazy man, and I swear he knows less about the way he plays the guitar than I know, and I swear I write my stuff exactly the way he plays the guitar. In short, we are brothers.

He is, strictly, at heart, one who knows. He knows all things. His knowing is sharp and swift and to the dead center of it all: he knows it is all death. He knows it is all nothing. He is a big, sorrowful-looking fellow in excellent

American clothes who plays the guitar the way I write.

Each time we meet at a party, this great Russian, this great singer who is truthfully my brother comes to me and very bitterly, in his deep voice, says to me, roaring deeply, very hurt about everything, a truly tragic man, a truly noble one, Wheelyam Sar-o-yan, *you* will understand.

I don't try hard to understand because it seems I almost always understand without trying, and I bust out laughing, and he tells me he cannot understand how I understand, how I write what I write. Sometimes, believing what I say, I say, sincerely but with a smile, that it is true, very often I do not know what I write, what I say. I simply write, something perhaps more significant than I know, which falls in place by itself, rather strangely. And oddly enough, or not oddly at all, he brings out his guitar, takes his stance, which is practically tragic, truthfully a thing to see and remember, and after a suitable half minute of reverent silence, he begins easily, effortlessly, as I begin each of my pieces, to sing and play the guitar. And before you know it, before you've had a chance to understand anything about anything he's singing and playing like one who was placed in this world to sing and play a guitar; and in no time at all the room is full of electrical, I might go so far as to say holy, splendor, magnificence, tragedy, and comedy; all at once, all together, all of it together in one piece. Eat, eat, eat, he sings in Russian, only the Russian word is not so flat, *kossi, kossi, kossi*. This Russian word for eat is the warm, kindly, gentle one of the mother to her child, the endearing one, *kossi, kossi, kossi*.

I do not believe there is a better singer of this kind in the world, nor for that matter, of my kind, a better writer. This man is possessed. And, unless I am badly mistaken, I am too. Most people meeting me, talking with me, do not get the impression that I am a great writer, and often do not believe me when I tell them so. Very often, even after I have told them six or seven times, they do not believe, and I beg them to read my stuff. I know they will know, while they are reading my stuff and afterwards that everything I have said to them is true, and I beg them because I know it will be a splendid and extraordinary and funny experience for them. To hear me bragging, and then to read my stuff and know that I *am* a great writer. I beg them to read my stuff, so it will be complete.

I admit it. I am possessed. Most of the time not violently so. But often enough. Not haunted, mind you. The presence is not an evil one. It is often angry and bitter and furious, but most of the time it is warm and friendly and amiable and gentle and courteous, and at times a little gallant, even. It is a good presence, and in varying degrees it is with me always. I do not mind it at all, and am on the contrary on excellent terms with it. We sometimes have quarrels. I am sometimes strongly inclined toward one thing, such as loafing and having an easy-going time, and this presence is inclined toward another thing, such as sitting down somewhere and putting two or three thousand words on paper, making a story, or something else. As I say, I do not know a great deal about what the words come to, but the presence is always anxious that I take time out to say something. I say, What's there to say? And the presence says, Now don't get funny; just sit down and say anything; it'll be all right. Say it wrong; it'll be all right anyway.

Half the time I *do* say it wrong, but somehow or other, just as the presence says, it's right anyhow. I am always pleased about this. My God, it's wrong, but it's all right. It's really all right. How did it happen?

Well, that's how it is. It's the presence, doing everything for me. It's the presence, doing all the hard work while I, always inclined to take things easy, loaf around, not thinking, not paying much attention to anything, much, just putting down on paper whatever comes my way.

The Russian singer told me about this. Wheelyam Sar-o-yan, he said, I know what you are saying, but *you do not know*.

This is, unfortunately, or fortunately, true. I think fortunately. Because I like being alive. And being dumb this way allows me to stay alive. By rights I should have died long ago. This is no fancy phrase. It is the truth. By all rights I should have died long ago.

Two years ago, at three in the morning, when I fell down a flight of cement stairs into the basement of a Greek restaurant on Market Street in San Francisco and should have been instantly killed, why did I get up and yell at Pete the short order cook, What the hell's the big idea putting these stairs where the toilet's supposed to be?

How did that happen? How did it happen that I was not even scratched?

I could give seventeen other instances. All those years,

all that crazy stuff, all those years when I had no money, why didn't I die? How did it happen that I didn't even lose my hair?

I have always suspected that what I am doing is not the work of one man, but I have never given the matter much thought. Then I met this Russian singer, and he told me, and now I know for sure.

The Same as Twenty Years Ago

On the way down we got thirsty and stopped at the first place on the highway just in time to hear the last few seconds of the fourth round of the Barney Ross-Henry Armstrong fight. I was swallowing root beer out of a bottle when I remembered it was the day of the fight and just about time it was going on. It was very hot, the way you don't mind particularly, because it brings you to life more truly than any other variety of climate. There was a paunchy, pleasant, middle-aged salesman of some sort in front of the radio with a bottle of beer in one hand and a cigar in the other.

That's how I knew it was the fight.

We stayed in this place on the highway until the fight was over. It was like I told them. No matter how they happened to be betting in the East, Armstrong would all but kill Ross, but Ross would stand up through each of the fifteen rounds.

When we got to Fresno it was early night and we were all hungry so we went into George's restaurant and had some more of the Armenian food. Jim had been eating the stuff four days in a row in Frisco, but wanted more. George was there, so we got special stuff, which was too good to resist, even though we didn't need it all. We sat around after dinner for half an hour, talking, and then Jim and Mike went on down to Hollywood, and I called up my cousin, the crooner of the vineyard country.

He came down in ten minutes and said the dirtiest word in the language.

What's the matter? I said.

Somebody stole both my guns, he said.

Today? I said.

No, he said. Two months ago. I haven't got any money to buy new guns with. Also, my girl is in love.

With somebody else?

No, with me, he said. I can't act natural any more. I've got to be nice all the time.

You're in a hell of a mess, aren't you?

I guess I'll get another girl.

Don't do it, I said. Stick with it a while and maybe you'll fall in love too and then both of you can suffer. Any new songs lately?

Couple.

Let's hear them, I said.

We went out and got in his car and drove out toward Skaggs Bridge. He sang two I'd heard three dozen times each over the radio in Frisco. He sang them better than the radio singers had ever sung them. Then he began talking like Roosevelt making a fireside chat in the summer.

My friends, he said, in 1931, under the administration of Herbert Hoover, the affairs of our country took a down grade. Under the present administration the affairs of our country have reached bottom.

Four years ago there were fifteen million unemployed, he said. Today there are *fifty* million unemployed.

All right, I said. Lay off that bad impersonating.

I'm a sadist, my cousin said. I'm the saddest guy in this town.

You're not so sad, I said.

Come out to the ranch tomorrow, he said, and watch me drive the new tractor.

O. K., I said. Let's go get a root beer.

We went back to town and up to the office where he slumped down in the swivel chair, put one leg over the arm of the chair, dangled his right arm out in space, and began to act.

Love, he said, and made a sick face that was somehow an exact approximation of the state of love.

Despair, he said and made the same face, with the same result.

Anger, he said, making the face again.

Bitterness, he said.

Scorn.

Delight.

Ecstasy.

Delirium.

Boredom.

O. K., I said, you've practically traveled the gamut, as they say.

Do you think I could get a job in Hollywood?

As far as I can tell, I said, you've got the job, except

that you don't do it in front of a camera, don't get paid, and can really act. Your version of ecstasy makes Dietrich look sick.

My cousin made the face again.

You mean like this?

That's right.

Righteous indignation, he said.

Hope.

Disgust, he said. How long you going to be in town?

A month maybe, I said.

Ten to one you leave by Saturday.

I don't call you, I said.

A little after four in the morning he came out to my grandmother's and woke me up and we had coffee together and drove out to the 160 acres where I watched him drag the harrow over the earth between the rows of Emperor vines. I ate two pounds of loquats and went down to the pond to scare up the frogs and be in a place I knew twenty years ago, before my cousin was born. The pomegranate trees along the road to the house were in blossom. The same birds were around and the same dragonflies were everywhere. It was fine to be alive and capable of all the conditions my cousin was so expert at approximating.

He quit work at noon and we drove back to town for a two-hour nap after a shower; then another shower and some food.

I've found an artist in a dump on G Street, near Chinatown, my cousin said.

What's he do? I said.

Piano, and sing.

Who is he?

Big colored boy, my cousin said.

Let's go hear him, I said.

Too early. We'll go for a ride, he said.

If you're going for a ride, his father said, go out to Riverdale and Huron for me.

No, my cousin said.

Sure, I said.

It's away over to hell and gone in the driest country in the world. It's out around Coalinga. It's too far.

What's the difference? I said. We've got all afternoon. His father named two places for us to visit and some information to get. We got in the Chrysler and started out.

It was the driest country in the world all right, but in a way awfully beautiful. At Huron we stopped at The Shack for beer and dropped nickels in the phonograph. The signs in the little dump were printed by somebody creative in that region and had a certain element of style. *Yourin Huron. It's all right for ladies to smoke cigarettes, but watch out where you lay your butts. What the hell are you looking in this corner for?*

The four women in The Shack ranged in age from thirteen to about sixty-two, I'd say, and were all dried-out, giddy, and immortal practically. I never felt greater affection for people than the affection I felt for these four.

On the way back to town we stopped every ten miles or so for root beer and music and a bit of a try at one or another of the marble games.

At one place I began putting pennies in a machine that gave you a half dozen candy-coated peanuts for a penny, and, with luck, a little bit of an item of some sort, such as a bear stamped out of lead, or a setter, or one dice. All I got was the candy, which I didn't want. The little unshaved man who owned the place was terribly displeased with the machine when, after putting in eighteen pennies, I didn't get one little bitty item.

Well, I'll be dipped in honey, he said with anger.

In the evening we went over to the place near Chinatown to hear the colored boy play the piano and sing. My cousin was right about him. He was truly an artist. We gave him four bits each and he played about an hour. He was especially good on *Hawaiian Hospitality* which he himself liked very much. He sang his own lyrics which were much better than the regular ones. When he sang *Trees* he said, Leafly Arms. He had a list of songs he knew well. One of them was, *You Be Long To Me*. I never did get around to asking him to play that one. He was a man of fifty who'd been with the best colored orchestras in the country in his day. He liked to drink, too. One night somebody handed him a glass full of something which he swallowed and then said, That was wonderful; what was it?

Milk, they told him.

Sure enough, I left town Saturday morning at six thirty.

The Russian Writer

In Russia I ran into a small, undernourished, high-strung, mournful-looking young writer who spoke better English than I do, only with an accent, and he said, Comrade, I have read everything. I have read many of your American writers. I know the works of John Dos Passos, Ernest Hemingway, Jack London, and many others. Still, I know nothing. I know nothing about anything. I am twenty-seven years old. I am a writer too. You are a writer too. Still, if I may say so, Comrade, do you know anything?

If memory serves, he was only an inch taller than a midget. He smoked one Russian cigarette after another, inhaled deeply while he talked, and even more deeply while he remained silent. The other Russian writers in that city were taller men, or fatter, or quieter, or dumber. One of them was a giant. This small writer told me this big one was the worst of the lot, although they were all bad.

Forgive me, he said, if what I say seems counter-revolutionary, but we are the worst writers in the world. We are the very worst. We are the ultimate of worseness.

Here, he said. Here are six of my books. You cannot read Russian, thank God. Look at the print. All of it is the worst writing in the world. Where is Chekov? Where is young Gorky? Where is Tolstoy? Where is Andreyev? Have they all died in us? I have read your stories, he said. You are a very bad writer. My God, you write badly, but everybody is not dead in you. You are not bad as we are. We are the way we are because they are all dead in us. In you two or three of the Americans are alive. That is why you are so bad. You are always jumping around because they are all so alive in you. My God, everything you write is awful, but it is much less awful than everything we write. Comrade, he said, do you know anything at all?

Well, I said, I know when it's raining.

So, he said. Again. Again you can laugh. It is not funny, though. *I* do not even know when it is raining. Yesterday the sun was shining and I sat in this room writing a story and I did not know the sun was shining. I thought it was raining. I tell you I thought it was raining all the time. It is because we are so sad. You have heard them laughing. It is false. Listen to them next time they laugh and you will know it is false. It isn't false when *you* laugh. It is crazy, but it isn't false. How can you laugh, Comrade?

I'll tell you an American joke, I said. It will make you laugh. I told him the one about the father and the beautiful daughter on the train to Cleveland that was held up by train robbers. You know the one. Where the father says, If only your mother had been here, Alice, we would have been able to save the luggage. Every time I tell this

story it makes me roar with laughter. Every time somebody else tells it I've got to laugh too. It's a great, goofy,
American joke. I laughed all over the room, and the young
writer went into hysterics, slapping his knee, bending
over, running around the room, and bumping his head
against the walls.

When he stopped laughing, there were tears in his eyes.

Did you hear me laughing? he said. Did you feel the
grief of that laughter? Do you know another?

I told him the one about the two Forty-Second Street
fleas that went out adventuring one summer night. Remember?

The little writer went crazy over this one. His face got
red from too much laughing and then suddenly he sat
down on the floor and began to cry.

My God, he said, we can't even laugh. Please forgive
me, Tovarich. Please tell another.

I knew a hundred more, but I didn't want to upset
him like this. If I had known these jokes were going to
upset him this way I wouldn't have told them. It was sad,
the way he laughed like a young American who'd spent all
his life in the slums of some big city; he sounded like a kid
who'd been brought up in the slums of New York or
Pittsburgh or Chicago or Frisco.

You must tell me a Russian joke, I said.

He looked at me with an amazed expression on his face.

A Russian joke? he said. We have no jokes. The people
do not make up such stories as these. We have some
comedy. There are many comical peasants, and many pom-
pous executives who are very funny to observe, but no

jokes. We do not tell jokes. We won't admit it, he said, but everybody is dead in us. We are the very worst writers in the world.

I told him I didn't believe it. Late that night I asked the other writers about him. They spoke of him with the humbleness of inferiors. He is a great writer, they said. He is one of the very greatest. We believe that he will be greater than Chekov. He is only a baby now. He writes like a crazy man.

That's what I thought, I told them.

That same night I left that city and continued my journey.

The Journey and the Dream

Nagasaki, Bull, Mr. Isaac, Dynamite, Hollywood Pete, and a kid in a leather coat who looked like a college student were playing stud when I walked into the joint with money burning holes in my pockets.

Well, said Bull. Where the hell have you been? Sit down and go broke.

Thanks, Bull, I said. I'll sit down, but I'll try not to go broke.

It was September, raining, and I had just come home from Europe and New York. Months ago when I got up from the game and left town, the players were sitting in the same seats they now occupied. Only Curley was out of sight.

Where's Curley? I said.

Nagasaki the Jap told me. Curley die, he said. Curley win big pot.

You're kidding, I said.

That's right, said Hollywood Pete. He tried to bluff out of that spot, but they called him.

Too bad, I said. Curley was O. K.

The best, said Bull. He broke me as many times as I tried to bluff him.

Waiter, I said. Perry the waiter came running over. Bring me some whisky, I said. I want to drink to the memory of Curley.

Make it three, said Bull. And then everybody at the table except the kid in the leather coat decided to drink to the memory of the old gambler.

I sat down, and Flash, the Irish tenor who used to sing in burlesque, came over to find out how much worth of chips I wanted to buy.

Where you been? he said.

I just got back from Russia, I said.

I was born in Russia, said Dynamite. He was a smart Jew.

What city? I said.

Kiev, he said.

I stayed at the Karl Marx hotel in Kiev, I said.

God damn it, said Dynamite. You ain't kidding, are you?

No, I said.

I left Kiev when I was ten years old, he said. How's the river? Dnieper.

Swell, I said.

Did you see Stalin? said Mr. Isaac. He was a little Jewish tailor.

No, I said. I went to see Russia. How's it going, Flash?

Bluffing the best way I know how, he said.

Bring me thirty dollars' worth, I said.

Fat Laramie was dealing and the first card he gave me

was the Ace of Spades, which was swell. Perry came back with the drinks.

To Curley, I said.

To Curley, said the gamblers.

The kid in the leather coat was sitting on my left. Who's this guy Curley? he said.

He used to play here, I said. Usually he sat in the chair you're sitting in now. He was a great guy.

That calls for a drink, said the kid. Bring me the same.

How old a man was he? said the kid to the players.

He was a young man, said Bull, himself over sixty.

He was in his sixties, I said.

What the hell killed him? said the kid.

Bad heart, said Hollywood Pete.

Well, said the kid, I'm sitting in his chair. I don't suppose the game stops when a player dies.

No, said Nagasaki. Game go on all the time, night and day.

Neither night nor day nor storm nor war nor revolution interferes with this game, said Dynamite.

Where'd you get that? said Fat Laramie.

It's the truth, ain't it? said Dynamite.

Where'd you get it, though? said Fat Laramie.

I'm not as dumb as some of the players around here, said Dynamite. I know when to retreat. I got it out of a book.

I thought so, said Fat Laramie. I thought it didn't sound natural. What you mean is, this game goes on all the time.

It's a good game, said Nagasaki.

Yeah, said Bull. You haven't worked in two years. You've been in this game two years now. You never lose, do you, Nagasaki?

Sometimes lose very bad, said the Jap.

Yeah, said Fat Laramie, I know.

Somebody's got to lose, said the kid in the leather coat. I'm about twenty dollars in the hole right now.

One night, said Bull, I saw Curley lose eighty dollars in one pot to Crazy Gus who was drunk. Gus drew out on him. Curley had aces back to back and Gus had treys back to back. Curley bet everything in front of him on the fourth card. He wanted the poor fool to know he had the best, but Gus was too drunk to know anything; or maybe drunk *enough* to know everything. Anyway, he called and made two pair.

That was tough, said the kid.

Wait a minute, said Bull. Curley fished into his pocket and brought out a quarter and a dime. He bought seven white chips. Two hours later Crazy Gus got up from the table broke, and Curley had all his chips.

That's *luck* for you, said the kid.

Luck nothing, said Bull. Curley knew how to play. They can draw out on you once in a while, but not all the time.

Mr. Isaac said something, then Nagasaki said something, and then Hollywood Pete, and one after another each of the players said something while the game moved along into the night and the year. It was great and I knew I was home again. Somebody went broke and got up and went away and somebody else sat down in his chair, and I began to forget everything. It was fine. It was perfect because I wanted to forget everything. I played the way the cards demanded that I play and the cards were full of kindness. They didn't race after me, and they didn't trick me.

It was a little after midnight, and I was home again from Europe. The streets of all the cities I had visited, and the people of these streets, and the words of the foreign languages, began to return to the wakeful dream, and I began to return to each place I had visited for a day, or an afternoon, or an hour, and I began to see again each face I had seen, each street, each configuration of city and village.

I knew I'd be playing poker till the journey ended. All winter, most likely.

I drank whisky all night and left the game sober and hushed early in the morning. I went into the cafeteria on the corner and ordered buckwheat cakes with bacon and hot coffee. Then I walked three miles to my room through rain. I took off my wet clothes and got into bed. I slept and dreamed the journey, almost wakening now and then to listen more consciously to the sound of the train rushing from Paris to Vienna, through the Swiss and Austrian Alps. To look more clearly upon the green fields of Europe. To breathe more deeply the clear cold air of dawn in Austria. And when I got up at three in the afternoon, I felt stronger and wiser and more melancholy than ever before in my life.

I was beginning to forget everything, and the only

way you can do that is to remember everything in the conscious dream and return everything to the living void of memory.

Then you'll be born again. Then you'll waken from the sleep of unbirth to the wakeful sleep of mortality.

The game lasted a long time, longer than the reckoning of days on the calendar, longer than time pulsing to inhale and exhale of breath, and the come and go of seatide, every moment wakeful and dreamed, inhabiting present and past, absorbing all movement over sea and continent, bringing the world together into one swiftly perceived reality and truth, and one morning when I got up from the game I knew the journey was ended and when I walked into the street I was laughing because it was so good to be in the world, so excellent to be a part of the chaos and unrest and agony and magnificence of this place of man, the world, so comic and tragic to be alive during a moment of its change, the sea, and the sea's sky, and London, and London's noise and fury, and the cockney's lamentation, the King's Palace, the ballet at Covent Garden, and outside Covent Garden the real ballet, and France, and the fields of France, and Paris, and the streets of Paris, and the stations, and the trains, and the faces, and the eyes, and the grief, and Austria, and Poland, and Russia, and Finland, and Sweden, and Norway, and the world, man stumbling mournfully after God in the wilderness, the street musicians of Edinburgh crying out for God in the songs of America, dancing after Him down steep streets, the tragic dream stalking everywhere through day and night, so that when I walked into the street I was laughing and begging God to pity them, love them, protect them, the king and the beggar alike.